PULP
Literature

PULP Literature

PULP LITERATURE PRESS

Issue No. 29, Winter 2021

Publisher: Pulp Literature Press; Managing Editor: Jennifer Landels; Senior Editor: Mel Anastasiou; Acquisitions Editor: Genevieve Wynand; Editor: Jessica Fabrizius; Poetry Editors: Daniel Cowper & Emily Osborne; Assistant Editors: Samantha Olson, Veronika Kos, Melisa Gruger, & Brooklynn Hook; Copy Editors: Amanda Bidnall & Mary Rykov; Proofreader: Mary Rykov; Graphic Design: Amanda Bidnall; Cover Design: Kate Landels; First Readers: Carol McCauley & Brenda Carre; Subscriptions: Carol McCauley; Advertising: Samantha Olson. For advertising rates, direct inquiries to info@pulpliterature.com.

Cover painting, *A Foundation of Lies* by Kris Sayer. Artwork for 'Blue Skies over Nine Isles' by Hugh Henderson. All other illustrations by Mel Anastasiou.

Pulp Literature: ISSN 2292-2164 (Print), ISSN 2292-2172 (Digital), Issue No. 29, Winter 2021.

Published quarterly by Pulp Literature Press, 21955 16 Ave, Langley, BC, Canada V2Z 1K5, pulpliterature.com, at $15.00 per copy. Annual subscription $50.00 in Canada, $68.00 in continental USA, $86.00 elsewhere. Printed in Victoria, BC, Canada, by First Choice Books / Victoria Bindery. Copyright © 2021 Pulp Literature Press. All stories and works of art copyright © 2020 their authors as per bylines.

Pulp Literature Press gratefully acknowledges the support of the Canada Council for the Arts.

Pulp Literature is a proud member of the Magazine Association of BC and Magazines Canada.

TABLE OF CONTENTS

FROM THE PULP LIT PULPIT

Winter Wonder

When staring down the blank page, a writer might turn to a writing prompt for inspiration. For this issue's editorial, that inspiration came from RH Blyth, who, when speaking of poetry, describes haiku as 'an open door that looks shut'. Well, if that doesn't beautifully capture the spirit of winter itself, I don't know what does.

Of all the seasons, winter is the most like a shuttered door. Leaves are off the trees, migratory birds have departed, snow blankets much of the landscape. It is as if Earth has put a finger to her lips and gently sighed, *Hush*.

But, of course, all is not as quiet as it seems. The roots of those trees are resting but ready, the birds are chirping elsewhere, and the snow on the rooftops is a temporary veil on the life that continues to buzz in the homes beneath.

Whether of words or winter, an open door that looks shut invites us to share in the creative process. To seek inspiration where none first seems to exist. To remember that even though something looks barren, great promise dwells on the other side.

When facing a new page, a new season, or a new year, we make a leap of faith that life will open itself to us. That all we need is already there, waiting, however quiet it seems. As the world welcomes a new year, we wish you health and peace, and the courage to nudge the door and begin again.

~Genevieve Wynand

*I*N THIS ISSUE
With *A Foundations of Lies* by cover artist **Kris Sayer**, we emerge from the dark woods with Tatterhood's loyal goat Bokki. Sword in hand (or mouth!), and fierce battle won, we are ready to take on the varied landscapes of this issue, no passport required.

In 'The Library Giant' by feature author **Shashi Bhat**, the struggle with nature—human nature—rages deep within. Meanwhile, in British Columbia and Iceland, ghosts of grief wander with the living as **KT Wagner**, **SL Leong**, and **Erin K Wagner** explore the rocky terrain of memory.

And whether in a culvert or factory, but most certainly within one's own mind, **Mike Gillis** and **Brandon Crilly** remind us how difficult it can be to navigate wreckage of the heart.

Forest, river, mountain, ocean—Mother Nature has a starring role in the winning stories for the 2020 Hummingbird Flash Fiction Prize: 'The Weeping Pools' and

'River's Thousand-One Voice' by **Cadence Mandybura**, and 'Glimpse of a Goddess' by **Laura Kuhlmann**.

Poets **Abner Porzio**, with 'Californian Illusion', and **Michael Penny**, with 'Kalaloch Beach, WA', introduce us to two very different wild west coasts.

Next, take flight and soar above it all with part three of **Joseph Stilwell** and **Hugh Henderson**'s comic saga *Blue Skies Over Nine Isles*.

And finally, heroines Frankie Ray and Allaigna enter danger-ous territory of their own as they search for clues to murder. In 'Sleuth With Star Quality' by **Mel Anastasiou**, Frankie Ray dons a disguise and braves a brothel. And in 'The Killing Ground', the second part of *Allaigna's Song: Oburakor* by **JM Landels**, Allaigna buries the dead in a blood-soaked wasteland.

Pulp Literature Press

THE LIBRARY GIANT

Shashi Bhat

Shashi Bhat's fiction has appeared in publications across North America. She was the winner of the 2018 Journey Prize. Her novel, The Most Precious Substance on Earth, is forthcoming from McClelland & Stewart in 2021. Visit her at shashibhat.com.

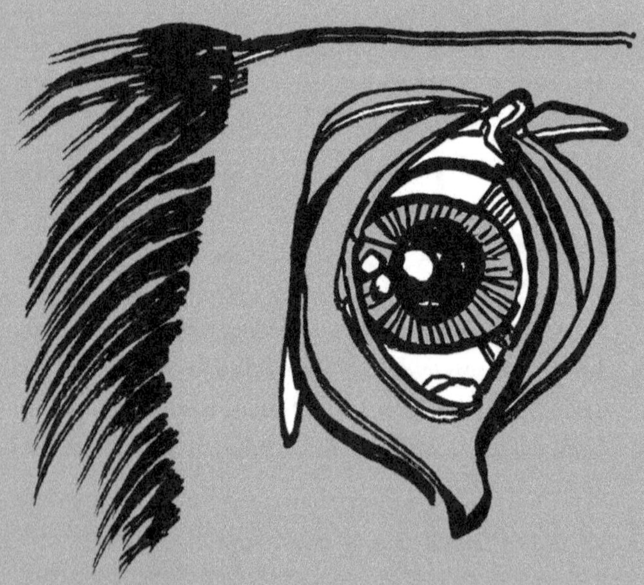

The Library Giant

He worked at the printing counter of the university library, ordering supplies, replacing printer toner, and helping students clear the jammed copier. He was precise, reading the instructions that flashed in the small digital window, then lifting and unlatching the indicated compartment of the machine, seeking out the trapped, crimped paper with his oversized hands. You had to be silent in the library, especially if you were a giant. He tried to stay on the carpet and wore rubber-soled shoes to minimize the sounds of his steps. When people were in the elevator with him, he stifled his breathing and hunched and curled his upper body, holding his hands together tightly in front of him — like a child wishing for something — to appear smaller, to leave the others more space.

But when the elevator halted abruptly, he was the only passenger inside. First, he waited. He tapped his toes but stopped when the elevator began to shake. He measured his options. He could press the alert button and ask for help. "It's me," he would say politely, "Martin. Please let me out." But he couldn't help how loud his voice was — his whispers were like the Halifax wind that rattled your windows and pushed you backward, turned your umbrella's spine inside out. He decided to be patient, because someone would eventually need the elevator and realize it was paused somewhere between the first floor and the fourth floor, where he had been headed to find a book to read during his break. He had a particular book in mind; it had won some big prize years ago, but more importantly, it came in large print for his tired, giant eyes. After an hour, he knew the elevator's insides intimately: its four mirrors, one cracked dramatically down the middle; its brown leather wainscoting; the soundproof stripes of its lower half; the ceiling fluorescents in square cages. Inside the light fixtures were dead insects, splayed like asterisks against the glass.

The lights in the elevator went off in a swift shock. He didn't know what time exactly because he had never found a watch to fit his wrist. Even after his eyes adjusted to the darkness, he couldn't discern one wall stripe from another. Did the lights turn off automatically at night, or had the whole building lost power? Had the world outside been destroyed? What if all that was left was this elevator, and him?

He had read an article once about ten people caught in an elevator halfway up the CN Tower. He had never been in an elevator with ten people — it would be impossible. They had waited and waited, breathing the second-hand air. They might have eaten each other if it had gone on any longer. Martin had seen it before, that moment of a human turning inhumane.

Here in the elevator, he was not exactly human, and not giant either; he belonged to the building's machinery. He was part of what existed in the middle of the building, in the gap between floors: steel framework, concrete, dust, empty space, like the unused space in an atom. When he grew (as he would inevitably if he stayed here long enough, whether he ate or not) he would pry open the elevator doors with his nails (nails he always trimmed so carefully with garden shears) and he would let his limbs grow down into the elevator shaft and out into the stacks, until at last he formed the building's core.

With this thought, he bravely pressed the emergency button. He pressed it again and again until the button left its imprint on his thumb, until the metal panel yielded a thumb-sized dent, and then he yelled, "I'm here! I need to get out!" and all the books in the building shook on their rickety, galvanized shelves, and a stack of printer paper from his own desk went cascading to the floor, and somewhere deep in the labyrinthine layout of private study rooms, a wall clock fell and shattered and lost the time. Martin removed his cardigan and clawed the mirrors, startled at the dim reflection of his steroidal face. He touched the flaw in the mirror, took a jagged hold, and then he was climbing, his custom-made shoes against the much-examined walls, his shoulders lifting the panel in the ceiling; he climbed, breathing loudly and sweating in the dark.

FEATURE INTERVIEW

Shashi Bhat

Pulp Literature: *In 'The Library Giant', we meet a man trapped in body and space — perhaps also in mind. Could you tell us about the inspiration for this piece?*

Shashi Bhat: The inspiration came from a couple of places. 1) I had read a scene somewhere (I can't remember where now!) about a man stuck in an elevator, and 2) someone I knew mentioned he was once nicknamed 'the Library Giant'. I wanted to write a story about a quiet, polite, unassertive person who, because of the body he was born in, can't help but take up space. And then I thought I'd place him in a catalyzing situation where he is forced to act. I was interested in the question of whether he's acting against his nature or embracing his true nature, and how this duality exists and clashes within him.

PL: *Congratulations on your 2018 Journey Prize win for 'Mute'! Could you tell us about the story and the moment you learned you had won?*

SB: Thank you! 'Mute' is about a young woman who moves to Baltimore for grad school and goes on a date where she starts to feel very uncomfortable. The character in the story is a bit like the Library Giant in that she's not always able to speak up even when she wants or needs to.

Winning the Journey Prize was unreal. They didn't tell us

in advance who had won, so I and the two other finalists were all sitting together in the audience at the Writers' Trust Awards, waiting to hear the announcement. I was preparing myself to not win, so when they called my name, I was a little bit in shock and very nervous given that it was an auditorium full of people whose books I'd read.

PL: As Editor-in-Chief at EVENT magazine, what excites you most about CanLit today?

SB: I have enjoyed seeing the surge in stories that blend genres. These days we're publishing a lot more stories that feature elements of science fiction or magical realism or fantasy, but that are still very human. It excites me to read pieces where the boundaries don't seem to be so rigid, where writers are taking risks.

PL: As a writing instructor, what do you most enjoy about working with new writers? What do you find the most challenging?

SB: I find the enthusiasm of new writers contagious and refreshing. What can be challenging is when aspiring writers read only a very limited range of works (in terms of genre, style, author demographics, etc), especially when there's a resistance to reading and writing outside of this comfort zone. My favourite things about teaching involve introducing students to texts they might not have encountered or explored on their own, and encouraging them to experiment.

PL: Are there any 'rules of writing' that you especially enjoy breaking?

SB: I think that 'show don't tell' is an interesting rule to test, because of course, it's reductive: a story involves an interplay between showing and telling. I like wrestling with what to keep on the page and what to leave off, whether to say how a character feels or let a reader intuit it. If we were always showing and never telling, a story would become long and tiresome; if we were doing the opposite, a story would just be a plot summary. Sometimes you have to just say what you mean, and sometimes you have to plunge the reader into the experience.

PL: Your work at EVENT allows you to walk the halls of creative non-fiction. Could you tell us a bit about the genre, and what makes for an exceptional creative non-fiction piece?

SB: I think the tagline of *Creative Nonfiction* magazine puts it accurately and succinctly: "True stories, well told." At *EVENT* we're looking for stories about real experiences that are shaped and styled as fictional narratives. The pieces I find exceptional are the ones that aren't necessarily about particularly dramatic or rare events, but that are described in aesthetically striking and emotionally resonant ways. The ordinary turned extraordinary. The personal turned universal.

PL: To which writers do you turn for inspiration? Are there any other forms, artistic or otherwise, that inform your work?

SB: There are a handful of short stories I keep returning to for inspiration: Amy Hempel's 'In the Cemetery Where Al Jolson is Buried', ZZ Packer's 'Brownies', Aimee Bender's 'The Rememberer', Jhumpa Lahiri's 'A Temporary Matter', Tobias Wolff's 'Bullet in the Brain', and others. These are ones I read when I was first trying to write stories myself. I also seek out books by authors who mix pathos with a sense of humour — Mona Awad, Raven Leilani, Souvankham Thammavongsa, and Elif Batuman are writers I've enjoyed more recently.

I like this question about other artistic forms—I find it helps me while writing to imagine the story as though it were a piece of music (I was a pretty big band geek as a teenager). I look for ways to create ebb and flow, emotional highs and lows. My piano teacher used to tell me that as long as you nailed down the beginning and the ending, nobody cared what you did in the middle. I do think this philosophy has carried over into my writing, though I try my best with the middles, too!

PL: I understand you hail from Ontario by way of Nova Scotia. What brought you to British Columbia? What keeps you here?

SB: I've moved around a bunch, and after Ontario I lived in the US for about a decade before getting a job in Halifax. I moved to the Lower Mainland six years ago for my current position teaching creative writing at Douglas College and editing *EVENT*. What keeps me here is that I've found a job that's a really good fit for me—I feel lucky to be in a line of work where I get to talk about what I love with people who are equally passionate about those things.

PL: What has been your experience as a writer during a pandemic? Do you have any advice for writers struggling to put words to the page right now?

SB: I found it really hard to write in the early months of the pandemic, and felt horribly guilty about it because there was a rare period after the teaching semester ended when I actually had the time to write, and I had a bunch of deadlines approaching. Before the pandemic, in the summers I would meet with other writers in cafés several days a week, and we'd each quietly work on our writing projects, and that was how I'd stay productive. At home by myself, it's much easier to take naps, cook myself elaborate meals, and spend hours exploring the 'Am I the Asshole?' subreddit. I'm not great at giving advice, but what helped me was going on lots of walks, listening to Conan O'Brien's podcast, and reading articles about how I should go easier on myself for not meeting my perfectionistic productivity goals while living in a dystopia.

PL: You are set to release your new novel, The Most Precious Substance on Earth *(McClelland & Stewart), in 2021. Could you tell us about it?*

SB: *The Most Precious Substance on Earth* follows a girl who experiences a traumatic event at her high school when she's fourteen and then grows up to become a high-school teacher. Thematically the book is about the ways a woman is conditioned to be silent, the long-lasting effects of trauma, and the moral responsibility teachers have towards their students.

PL: Thank you for making the time to speak with us. One last question: What are you working on now?

SB: Thank you for these thoughtful questions! I'm working on my next book, a short story collection. Many of the stories are themed around the body—health and illness, bodily autonomy, and so on. Some of the stories border on the strange (allegorical, magical, surreal) while being grounded in real-world settings and themes, similarly to 'The Library Giant'.

THE EXTRA: FRANKIE RAY, SLEUTH WITH STAR QUALITY

Mel Anastasiou

Mel Anastasiou writes the Fairmount Manor Mysteries, starring Mrs Stella Ryman; the Hertfordshire Pub Mysteries, starring Spencer Stevens; and the Monument Studios Mysteries, starring Frankie Ray and Connie Mooney. She teaches the 'Standout First Page' segment of Pulp Literature Press's writing school, Quit the Day Job, and she wrote the steampunk-themed The Writer's Boon Companion: Thirty Days Towards an Extraordinary Volume *and* The Writer's Friend and Confidante.

Camillo's

The Extra:
A Monument Studios Mystery

Previously . . .

Hollywood, April 1934. Hollywood's most wanted 'murderess', Frankie Ray, is determined to employ all her acting chops to hunt down the murderer of movie star Gilbert Howard and clear her own name of the crime. She has two clues: testimony from the unreliable actress Billie Starr, and an unnamed witness who was Gilbert Howard's secret lover. Now, disguised as a suave male detective, Frankie tracks Billie into one of Hollywood's brothels.

Chapter One

Frankie landed with a grunt on the floor of Billie Starr's bedroom. Overhead, a flock of brilliantly-coloured Chinese kites dangled from strings tacked to the ceiling. Embroidered cushions lay about the bed and the floor as if Billie were expecting a lot of visitors from the Far East. Billie, cross-legged atop the neatly made bed in the middle of the room, shut her book with a snap.

It was one of Frankie's favourites: *Anne of Green Gables*.

Frankie hauled herself to her feet. "Don't be afraid, Billie. My name is Frank Achilles. I'm a friend."

It was only four o'clock in the afternoon, but Billie was not one to observe the cocktail hour. She picked a bottle up from the floor beside the bed and took a drink.

She said, "Young man, you must be cuckoo. You're not my friend. I've never seen you before in all my born life. And what do you mean by coming in through the window? Why didn't you just knock?"

Frankie said, "I did knock."

Billie said, "You didn't."

And meanwhile the manhunt was on. Frankie let out a hissing breath. "You're right. I shouldn't have gotten carried away climbing on rooftops and risking my neck. But I'm trying to help a mutual friend of ours, and I need you to answer a question about Gilbert Howard's death."

"Poor old Howie." Billie drooped visibly over her bottle. "What mutual friend are you talking about?"

"Our mutual friend, Frankie Ray." Frankie held her shoulders wide and her chin straight and manly. "Frankie's accused of killing Gilbert Howard."

"Frankie!" Billie exclaimed, and for a terrible moment Frankie was certain the girl had recognized her and was calling her by name. And if Billie, in her cups, could pierce her disguise, a policeman ought to know her a block away.

To Frankie's relief, Billie went on, "*Frankie* didn't kill him. What empty noggin thought up that idea?"

"Then who killed Gilbert Howard, Billie? When you first saw his body, you said—or rather, Frankie said that you said—that you knew who had killed him."

Billie blew an empty, hollow note across the top of her bottle. "Anybody would know *who*."

"Then, for heaven's sake, *who?*"

Unfairly, frustratingly—yet somehow inevitably—the door to Billie's room opened and the Chinese kites overhead swung and rattled. The house madam opened Billie's door, left it ajar, and vanished with an air of studied tact.

Frankie buttoned up her jacket. She wanted to growl like King Samson, *What now?* She half expected Billie's mysterious *friend in high places* to appear, or else the cops.

Marietta Valdes, still barefoot and carrying her shoes, sauntered into Billie's room. King Samson strode in close behind her. He said, "Be quick, Marietta. I've got no goddamn time to spare."

Marietta, said, "*There* you are, Billie."

Billie threw herself at the taller woman the way a child rushes to its mother's arms. A sudden, fierce sense of reunion charged the air.

"I thought you'd never come," Billie said to Marietta. "Will you get me out of here?"

"It's about time, too." Marietta nodded sharply. "We're going across the way. To the studios. This is my kid sister," she told King Samson.

"Pleased," King Samson said. He didn't sound pleased.

"Can we really go to Monument Studios? Without asking anybody?" Billie darted a look at King Samson, who glared back.

King Samson's sarcasm grew as thick and dark as his well-trimmed eyebrows. "Marietta gets everything she wants. Didn't you know that?"

"If only that were true," Marietta replied.

Frankie stared from Marietta to Billie and back again. How did sisters lose track of each other so completely? One hiding in a brothel, one in full view of the world in the movies! But then, Frankie herself had lost track of Connie in no time at all.

Samson said, "Marietta, I'll be damned if I'll screen-test your every relative and acquaintance, no matter what you say."

"I'll get Billie cleaned up, Sammy, and you'll talk out of the other side of your face," Marietta said. Until this moment, Frankie might not have been in the room. Now, with a jerk of her head, the actress said to Samson, "Meanwhile, you just work things out with Frank Achilles, the way we discussed."

Marietta shot the studio head a warning look, and led her sister out of the room.

The door slammed behind her, setting the kites spinning.

Samson batted at a dragon kite tail. He pulled it down and tore it across the wings. "All I want is control over my own goddamn film in my own bloody studio," he said. "Is that too much to ask?"

Frankie raised her eyebrows. What a heel King Samson was. But, he did have a right to run his own movie business.

"Worse, I've got to manage this rotten cast." Samson moved about Billie's room, yanking more kites down from the ceiling by their strings and tossing them on the floor. "I hired two of the biggest stars in the world to head up *The Emperor of New York*. One of them Gilbert Howard! A manipulative bastard, completely uninsurable, who now gets himself murdered. And as co-star I sign Marietta Valdes, who always has to know best about my movie and won't even take an engagement ring from me."

Frankie said, "Life is a bed of rocks, I guess."

"You got that right. Now, Marietta says, *Frank Achilles has got something. And he's a new face. And, with his colouring, he'll look wonderful up close next to me.* Hell! She's right, though."

Frankie started. Right about what? About *Frank Achilles?*

The producer was interested in her as a leading man. Ye gods and little fishes, her dream of being *discovered* was coming true, right here and now. She'd always daydreamed about being "discovered" by a producer or a director as she was riding a bicycle, or perching on a stool at a drugstore counter, sipping a milkshake. Never once had she imagined being offered a screen test while wearing a man's disguise. In a brothel. She sighed, and then vowed that, since she had to turn him down, at least she would do her utmost to enjoy every minute.

Samson said, "You've got something new about you, I guess."

Frankie replied breezily, "Well, then, I'm like a hundred thousand other new faces. *I'm* nothing special."

"You're right about that," Samson said. "But no actor is anything special, until somebody like me gets his hands on him."

"That so?" If Frankie had been wearing her true identity, and not a gentleman's grey suit and brogues, she'd never lie like she was lying now. "Well, I have no great desire to be a movie star anyway. All that glamour could get on a fellow's nerves."

Samson glared. "Can you act?"

Frankie proved that she could act, by drawling, "Are you really going to let *me* decide how to answer that question?"

"You've got that right, as well." Samson shot Frankie a nasty look. "I got a more important question: Can you handle Marietta Valdes for me?"

Manlike, Frankie shrugged.

Samson nodded. "Then I'll test you, since you seem to be a fellow who can take no for an answer, if you're lousy on film."

"I can *give* no for an answer, too." Frankie wished for a hat, to tilt it over one eye. "So here goes: nope. Don't want a screen test. Thanks, though."

"Don't argue with me." King Samson shook his head. "I hate men who argue all the time. Look at that damned Gilbert Howard, God rest his soul."

"I like a good argument, myself." It occurred to her that her current plight—being sought for murder—was a sort of life-and-death argument as well, some of it with the newspapers and some of it with the police. She added, "I lived with an arguer all my life—my dad. Anyway, isn't everything you see on the silver screen an argument—all those actors and actresses suffering and kissing and battling and rescuing? With the hero carrying the day during the ninety-minute black-and-white debate?"

"A smart guy." King Samson snorted. "Like I need one when I've got Marietta Valdes. You'll test. Come on." Samson opened the door. "And less of the backchat when I'm trying to do you a favour."

Like a bolt, Frankie saw that Samson was absolutely on the nose. He was offering her a vital opportunity to follow Billie inside the studios and question her again. She advised herself to keep up her cool attitude, as it was clearly working perfectly on King Samson.

"A screen test offer is not much of a favour," Frankie replied. "I'm a busy man."

"You know what, Achilles? I guess I don't need you after all." Samson spun round and left the room.

Frankie stared after him, feeling sick. She was an actor, all right. She'd just acted herself right out of grilling Billie about Gilbert Howard's murder. Now, she would have to rely on Eugene to find the golden swimmer that Frankie, Connie and Tom had seen with Gilbert Howard just before he was killed. Without a name, address, or even a better physical description than *slender, blonde, and naked,* that other girl witness was definitely a shakier prospect.

Frankie followed Samson out Billie's door and trotted after him past the numbered doors in the upstairs corridor.

To the producer's back she said, "I'd probably photograph poorly. Sure as shooting, a screen test won't come to anything."

"Like *you'd* know, you're such an expert." Samson faced Frankie at the top of the curved staircase. "Just shut up, fella, and get your grey-suited caboose over to my studio. Tell Marietta I said to go ahead and do the test."

And now the big thing was not to allow Samson to guess how relief sent the blood rushing around her head, arms, and legs. She paused for a count of three. "I guess I can give you an hour or two, if it means that much to you."

"Thanks so very much," Samson said, ironic as Alexander Pope.

"It's your nickel." As she followed him to the stairs, Frankie schooled her features into an expression of calm disinterest.

She trailed King Samson down the staircase to the brightly lit foyer, covering her smile, but also aware of a nasty sinking feeling inside. She was still trailing after Billie Star, looking for answers. Billie Starr! Who was perhaps — after Gilbert Howard himself — one of the least dependable people on the face of the earth.

Chapter Two

A Publicity fellow in a pinstriped suit jumped at Samson's order. He slotted Frankie in for the last screen test of the afternoon, and led Frankie along winding corridors to Make-up. She found herself in a little room that smelled like no room Frankie had ever been in before. Perfumery would be below Frank Achilles's notice, of course, but as a woman Frankie wanted to bury her face in all the blowsy, bosomy scents, as thick and un-French as porridge. Instead, she hurried to smear on her pancake foundation before the make-up artist, Leda, could snatch the tin from her. Frankie's jaw line was square enough to pass as male, but her chin was far too smooth for a man of her purported age, even one who had Burma-Shaved his face before setting himself down in Make-up's shiny mint green chair.

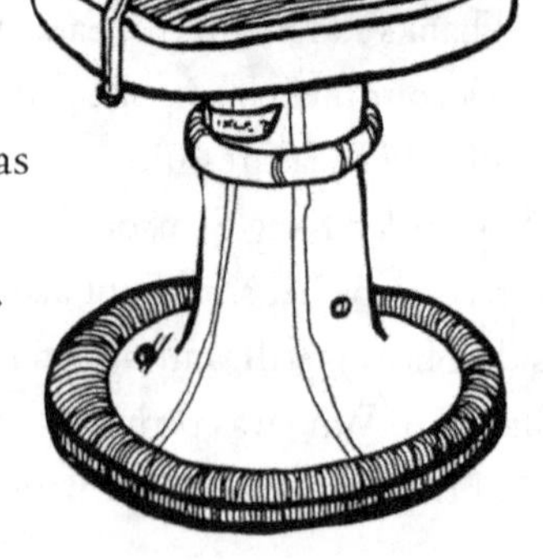

"It's like this," Frankie explained to a scowling Leda. "I do my own shaving and make-up, just like all the other men do."

"They most certainly do not. You have your job, Mr. Achilles, which you got by being born photogenic. I have mine, which I got by training as a professional."

Leda's logic was inarguable. What was worse, Frankie was achingly aware of the irony of her present situation. For years she had dreamed that a professional make-up artist would improve her face. Now Monument Studios was doing for Frank Achilles exactly what Frankie Ray had despaired of. She couldn't decide which was worse — to dream of being "discovered" by a movie producer and never have the dream come true; or to be "discovered," but as somebody else, *viz.* her alter ego, the non-existent Frank Achilles. What made the whole thing truly unbearable was that as Frank Achilles, she didn't have the time to make a good test. She must find Billie. She'd already been sitting here at Leda's mercy for ten minutes. How long until she might make her escape?

She eyed the door. Marietta might have taken Billie anywhere inside Monument Studios, but here in the central building was as good a place as any to begin looking for her.

Leda crossed her arms over her mint-green smock, which was the same colour as the mint-green walls. The colour-matching between employee and décor should have been charming but actually the effect was to make Leda's head appear from certain angles to be floating freely above the ground. "Young man, we're in a Depression, if you hadn't noticed. Are you trying to rob me of my job?"

"I won't tell if you don't." In case Leda's sharp eye had noticed how superhumanly smooth her chin was, Frankie chanted softly as she smoothed peach-coloured paste along her cheek, *"Does your husband misbehave? Grunt and grumble, rant and rave? Shoot the brute some Burma-Shave.* Maybe you saw the ads on the drive south, flicking by, little red signs on the road?"

"No."

"Burma-Shave works like a dream," Frankie added. She gave her own cheek a slap. "Smooth as Shakespeare. Listen, Leda, how about a glass of water for a fellow? Please."

But instead of leaving Frankie alone in the room to make her escape, Leda opened a cupboard and took out a glass. She slid aside a panel on one of the counters and revealed a hidden sink. She turned on one of the taps.

Darnital. Frankie would have to send Leda farther afield. "How about a sandwich, too?" She herself liked a cucumber sandwich with butter, salt and pepper, but that was strictly female fare. However, she well knew Champ's collation of choice and swiftly added, "Roast beef, please. With horseradish." It was becoming easier and easier to act like a man.

"Anything else you want? Champagne from a golden fountain?"

Frankie laughed appreciatively. "You oughta be in pictures, Leda," Frankie said. "You're a pretty funny gal."

Leda huffed through her nose. "With your attitude, you'd better be famous soon, kid. Sure, I'll get you a sandwich. But you'll have to wait. The cafeteria isn't open for another hour."

Frankie pictured every man she'd ever been acquainted with, at school and in church back in Vancouver. She tried to recollect how each left a room. It seemed that there was only one believable pretext remaining for a fellow to take his leave of a lady. Frankie got up from her chair "Leda, I love you dearly ..." What was Champ's phrase for *spend a penny?* "... but I gotta see a man about a dog."

"Get along with you, cheeky," Leda said, but she showed the first signs of a smile.

Frankie snatched up her jacket, tipped Leda a Boy Scout salute, and slipped by her into the empty corridor. As an afterthought she tugged off her make-up bib and dropped it behind one of the tall steel ashtrays dotted at intervals between doors along the hallway. Which way to find Billie? Frankie shrugged and turned right. The weight of the gun in her pocket set it swinging with each brisk step she took as she made her way, trying doors at random and finding them locked. She took side trips up a short corridor opening off the main way and found herself cornered in a cul-de-sac by a small stand of mops upright in buckets. Wrong turn.

Back in the main hallway, Frankie found a door that opened when she tried it. Billie wasn't there, but the door opened into a space thick with chrome wardrobe racks hung about entrancingly with clothing rich in colour and texture. These were the magic articles of fancy dress that transformed you. She wanted to stroll along the racks and run her hands over the fabrics. Instead, she shut the door firmly on all that silken and spangled glory. But someday she'd come back, dressed as herself. She swore to it with one of her father's irrevocable ministerial oaths.

Seven or eight locked doors later, at the end of what seemed an interminable corridor, Frankie came upon a door marked "Make-up 3." Without much hope, she tried the knob. When it turned, she peered in at a sky blue room where Billie Starr sat at a sky blue vanity table, finger-combing her honey-coloured hair. To Frankie's relief, the room contained no sky blue attendant.

"Now look here, Billie—" Frankie began but was brought up short by the calibre of swear word Billie let off.

"Frank Achilles! It's always the same, isn't it?" Billie said. "Hurry up and wait forever. Why, oh why, didn't I at least bring a flask? Have *you* got one?"

"Certainly not. Darn it all, Billie, I figured you drank so much because you didn't get into the movies. I thought you'd be glad as a dog with two tails once you got past the studio doors."

With Billie, you never had to wait for her to change gear.

"I *am* pleased to be inside the studio," Billie's smile was so sweet that Frankie couldn't understand how this perfect girl had failed to be signed to a studio in the first place. "I just want my flask, that's all."

Frankie thanked her stars that she had spent her entire life around Sheridan B. Ray and Connie Mooney, and thus was capable of keeping her temper. She looked sternly down at the young actress. "Billie, you must listen to me. Your unlucky friend Frankie Ray — remember her? Frankie? She's in trouble. The cops and the papers think she murdered Gilbert Howard. If you want to help her, answer me a couple of questions."

"Okay." Billie gazed up at Frankie. "And you answer me this: how do you think I'd look as a brunette?"

Frankie answered, "You'd look like what you are — Marietta's younger sister."

"Who told you she's my sister?" Billie demanded. "How would you possibly know that?"

Billie had already forgotten the scene in the brothel. What an awful witness she was. But she was still Frankie's best clue. "I'm a detective. Remember? So, I know things." When Frankie saw the wonderment in Billie's eyes, she knew it was time to strike. "Here's what you need to tell me, and quickly. When you and Frankie, she ..." All these nouns and pronouns were confusing, especially in a room that was all one colour — this one had a sky-blue floor, walls and ceiling, which made you wonder which way was really up. "When you and Frankie discovered Gilbert Howard's body on the sofa ..."

"Oh, Howie! I'll be heartsick for him, even in heaven." A tear shone in Billie's eye and she blinked it away. "I *won't* cry. He'd be the first to say not to. I haven't had a single still photo taken yet."

Out in the corridor, rapid steps neared and stopped outside the sky-blue make-up room door. Frankie held her breath. The footsteps moved on.

"Please hurry up and answer my question," Frankie begged. "Who killed Gilbert Howard? You said it was obvious."

"How do I know that you're really on Frankie's side?" Billie appeared suddenly as sober as she had been by the side of Gilbert Howard's dead body. "You could be a cop, out to arrest her."

Frankie flung out her arms. "Do I look like a policeman?"

"You look like a dreamboat, and that's so unfair to me." Billie twisted in her chair. "You're such a dreamboat of a man that Marietta is determined to get you a big starring offer. *I* am a dreamboat woman, but nobody helps me. Even Marietta, my own sister, says she can't do much for me. A few stills, and then it's out the door with a *Hey dee Hoo dee Hee.* Everything everywhere is easier for men."

Frankie had been a man for several hours now, and she was beginning to doubt this truism. "Billie, let's forget about stardom for a minute and think about poor old Frankie, accused of murder. You told her you know who killed Gilbert Howard."

Billie screwed her pretty features into an incredulous expression. "Who doesn't know who killed him?"

"Tell me who did it," Frankie said sternly.

"That I will. And then you'll know. And our friend Frankie will be all right, because of course Frankie didn't kill him."

Instinct and logic made Frankie hold her breath. Experience advised her not to interrupt. But what were instinct, logic or experience when pitted against the likes of Billie Starr? Billie was, after all, Marietta's sister. She folded her arms and tilted her head winningly. "I'll tell you when you help me."

A little less calmly, Frankie said, "We need to help *Frankie.* I thought she was your friend, Billie."

"Gilbert Howard was my friend, too, and he is dead," Billie said.

"How good a friend?" Frankie asked. "Too good a friend?"

"Keep your mind out of the gutter, please. Howie was the only one who stood by me when Leo wouldn't go to his famous parents to help me star in the movies. If not for Howie, I would never have had the brilliant idea of hiding out in a brothel."

"That's one heck of a good idea, I don't think! Why in heaven's name would Gilbert Howard tell you to go to a brothel?"

"Well, Howie used his influence to get me a private room with the madam—no visitors. Except Leo. Howie said that Leo would do anything to rescue the woman he loves from the brothel. Howie said that Leo would finally stand up to his father, King Samson, and get me a movie contract, and stand up to his mother, Blanche Carver, and get me some newspaper coverage—"

"Howie said!" Frankie shook her head. "Did you do everything that fellow told you to do?"

Billie laughed. "Don't you know? Everybody did."

Every female did. In fact, Frankie had as well, for Gilbert Howard had changed her life when he told her that he had been a schoolteacher like her and urged her onward to an acting career. And had changed her life again by turning up dead on her sofa.

"Billie, who killed Gilbert Howard?"

"You may look like a matinee idol, but you don't hear so well, do you, Frank Achilles? I said, I'll tell you when you help me."

"Darn you, Billie!" Frankie took a deep breath. "Help you how?"

The make-up chairs were of the expensive swivelling sort, and Billie swivelled in hers now. She held up her slender index finger to make a number one. "After the screen test, the studio is supposed to send me out to somewhere like a nightclub or a fancy restaurant on a date with a fellow like you, to put me in the public eye. First, lots of photographers take my picture. Then a columnist from one of the papers will speculate on my future and my past. Also, everybody there will see me dine with a man who is a bright new face in the movies. And then the next morning, my name is in the papers." Billie was counting off the steps on her fingers. "After that King Samson or somebody like him offers me a contract and a speaking role. It's a series of logical steps, do you see?"

"And where do I fit into all this?"

"The bright new face at the studio, that's you." Billie nodded at the door. "Go see Publicity. Get me a date with you tonight. And put me on the road to a very good part."

It was not so much the transaction itself that worried Frankie, as Billie's follow-through with her promise.

"All right. I'll keep my word, Billie. But don't forget yours. At dinner, on our date, tell me who killed Gilbert Howard."

Billie smiled, bright and golden as a Monument Studios angel. "Frank, you're a decent fellow. And I know you'll keep your word. So, I'm going to tell you who killed Howie right now."

Halfway out the door, Frankie turned and stared. A free gift of an answer? From Billie Starr?

Frankie said, "I'm listening."

"It's perfectly simple."

Frankie's heart hammered.

"Listen good," Billie said. "King Samson killed Howie."

The bully. King Samson. The producer's name chattered in Frankie's head, and she spoke through it with difficulty. "Billie, that can't be. Why would King Samson kill Gilbert Howard? Samson owns and controls Monument Studios. Everybody knows that King Samson is like an emperor around here. Why on earth would he risk his kingdom to kill a star who makes him money and brings him good reviews?"

"I guess you don't know a thing about the movie business, Frank Achilles. King Samson killed Howie for the insurance."

"But Gilbert Howard was uninsurable," Frankie said. "Killing him wouldn't bring Samson a dime. In fact it would lose him money by setting movie production back."

Billie frowned. "Well, then, Samson killed Howie because he hated him." She returned Frankie's gaze with an expression of sincere compassion. In those blue eyes Frankie read the message clearly: Billie Starr believed Frank Achilles was a gullible sap.

"You don't suspect Samson at all, do you?" Frankie asked. She could only think of two people that Billie would want to protect, and one of them—Billie's sister Marietta Valdes—had no motive. But the other person had lost Billie to the brothel, under Gilbert Howard's encouragement.

Frankie said, "It was Leo you thought of when you saw that Gilbert Howard was dead, wasn't it?"

Billie shook her head.

Frankie pressed. "You believe that Leo shot Gilbert Howard, don't you? Not because Howard shot Leo at the audition in Vancouver, but because Gilbert Howard sent you, the woman Leo loves, into the brothel."

Billie made a baby-face pout and turned away. At the same moment, the door to the sky blue room slammed open. Marietta Valdes strode into the room. She was decked out in the most outrageous silver dress Frankie had ever seen, on screen or off.

"Leo most certainly did not kill Gilbert Howard." Marietta Valdes seemed to float within her dress, which resolved itself into an unthinkable number of silvery feathers. The star's makeup bib was tucked neatly around her neck. "I admit freely that I was listening at the door just now. Frank Achilles, you need to understand that what looks like a complex sin in the little towns we all come from is simple acting in Hollywood. The camera observes but does not judge, so that the viewer can bring her own ethics to the case. Don't you think?"

"I don't know." Frankie did her best to cover her befuddlement. She fished her sunglasses out of her pocket, put them on, and felt better. Smarter. "I'll have to think about that one."

Marietta turned to her sister. "Billie, only an idiot would accuse King Samson of murdering his own star."

Billie turned her chair around and scowled into the mirror.

Frankie took a step nearer Marietta. "Miss Valdes, you knew Gilbert Howard. Knew him well?"

"And liked him! Better than most."

"Then if not King Samson, or his son — and if not Frankie Ray — then who do you think killed him?"

Marietta said, "Every woman he ever met killed him."

A sinking feeling crept over Frankie. The motive for Howard's murder — the revenge of women seduced, scorned and betrayed — was strong, and the cast of suspects long. However, as far as the papers, the public, and the law were concerned, whose name would be written at the top of that particular list? Frankie Ray's — even though Gilbert Howard had neither broken her heart nor smashed her virtue. All he had done was recite soaring prose by the side of a pool and urge Frankie to follow her dreams.

Frankie took a step back. "Miss Valdes, are you telling me that every woman Howard ever met wanted to shoot him, except you? In the whole wide world of his romantic adventures, you're the only woman who never wanted to kill him?"

"I was never one of his conquests." Marietta smoothed the silver feathers that made up her dress. "Howie saw me as his equal in the professional field. He was my best chance at directing. Now, go away, Frank Achilles. I'll see you again, soon enough." Marietta swirled out the door.

Billie said, "So, will you keep your promise, Frank Achilles? Like I kept mine?"

Frankie said. "I don't believe a word you said, but I did make you a promise. Which way is Publicity?"

"That-a-way." Billie jerked her head to the right and swivelled her chair around to face the makeup mirror.

Frankie strode manfully along the hallway in the direction Billie had indicated, trying to appear self-confident while feeling completely let-down. Still, she had never, at any time in her life, seriously contemplated giving up on anything or anybody. She had never even lost hope that her mother might one day return to the blue house to see how her daughter Francesca was getting along. She would not give up now. She reached the door labelled *Publicity.* It opened to reveal a sharp-looking fellow in a green tweed suit. Behind him on a small desk stood two large telephones.

Frankie told publicity what she wanted.

Publicity chewed his lip. "You telling me my job?"

"Just this once."

"Okay, sport. I'll do what you ask today. And, after that you're in my pocket on a permanent basis. You'll go where I send you. Deal?"

Frankie nodded. "My word on it."

"Okay, meet Miss Starr outside Camillo's Fine Bar and Grille on Sunset Boulevard at eight pip emma. Your first acting job is to look romantic."

"How?"

Publicity rolled his eyes. "You're an actor, aren't you? Now show me your profiles."

Frankie showed Publicity both her profiles. "Is one better than the other?"

"How I love a greenhorn. Your right profile is a bit on the feminine side. Always have the photogs snap your left. Any questions?"

Frankie did, but they weren't the kind she could ask Publicity. *Who killed Gilbert Howard? Was it the golden girl, as she'd always suspected? A jealous Leo Samson? A wronged woman, as Marietta insisted?*

The pot of suspects was too large. Gilbert Howard must have left a trail of envy and broken hearts clear across the city. His murderer might have been a heartbroken actress, a resentful character actor, a disappointed fan, a passing maniac … or a girl he'd talked into living in a brothel. Or the sweethearts or spouses of any of those.

Frankie herself did have plenty of motive, just as the police and Blanche Carver believed. And so did the one person Frankie least wanted to suspect of the crime. Her best friend, Connie Mooney, had disappeared the very day that Gilbert Howard's body was found in Villa 7B. But Frankie knew Connie as well as she knew herself. Connie wouldn't kill anybody. And if she did kill somebody, she wouldn't let Frankie take the blame. So that gave her two people to rule out—Connie and herself—among the many suspects.

She traced her path the along the snaking halls of Monument Studios' central building and reflected on Sherlock Holmes, who, with daring, logic, and disguise, could accomplish more than Scotland Yard and its numbered investigators. Like Dr. Watson, Frankie had always admired Holmes above other detectives. But she decided that when you had a city full of suspects, logic, intuition, and experience were useless. You needed a great army of policemen.

She experienced a sudden dizziness, along with a strange and terrible sense that something was about to fall on her from a great height. She looked up, but there was nothing above her but the spackled white ceiling of the studio corridor. Still, something washed over her from her platinum head to her brogue-shod feet. It was wet and chilly, and its name was Common Sense.

Frankie shivered. The soles of her manly brogues tapped against the seemingly endless corridor flooring. She passed doors on each side with little plates reading *Writer, Editor, Assistant Writer, Casting.* She wondered how she had ever believed she could solve a murder by dressing up in a man's clothes. She put her right hand in her pocket and wrapped it around the gun, hoping for a little cold, hard comfort.

Chapter Three

Frankie drove the Model A along Sunset Boulevard under a starry evening sky. She frowned through the windshield at the road ahead. Lord, how she hoped Billie was wrong and that the killer wasn't King Samson. Frankie had no wish to bring down Monument Studios and all the people Samson employed—actors, extras and all the others lucky enough to have jobs in this place. Tom and the kids from Paradise Gardens—and Bruno!—and Luigi the cameraman, who'd helped her do so well as the sad pigeon girl. Frankie would never do anything to take away their chance to make their mark in life. Still, of all the people Frankie had met, who had the worst temper? Who was most likely to explode out of control? And who owned the cursed gun in her pocket that had killed the movie star in the first place? King Samson.

But such reasoning was instinctive, like Billie herself. Frankie was determined to be sensible. King Samson was a terrible bully, and impossible to like, but he couldn't be Gilbert Howard's killer. Samson's film project depended on the uninsurable star Howard showing up on set and camera-ready. Samson needed Howard alive.

Billie's conclusion was certainly not worth the price Frankie had promised her. But here was Frankie anyway, dressed as a man and risking exposure with every moment she spent on the street, all in order to give Billie Starr her opportunity to be seen and photographed on a warm Hollywood evening at Camillo's Fine Bar and Grille. As Frankie pulled up to the curb around the corner from Camillo's she was satisfied that she was doing the right thing in helping Billie. However, the fates offered no reward for virtue and honesty tonight, because when she stepped down from the Model A, a policeman stopped her.

Her heartbeat stuttered and nearly stopped. She'd known this moment would come. Still, she wouldn't allow her internal biology to bring about discovery and downfall. She was an actress. So, she would act.

She reminded herself that Eugene, much like this policeman, was also asking questions around Hollywood, searching for the golden swimmer, the girl that had last been with Gilbert Howard. Perhaps, by now, Eugene had found her.

Frankie put one hand casually into her suit pocket and touched the gun she carried there. She said the words an innocent man would say: "Yes, officer?"

"Have you seen this girl, pal?" The policeman, a heavyset fellow, held out a glossy photograph. "Take a look, wouldja?"

The first thing was not to answer too eagerly. Frankie breathed in and out, as one did at the beginning of acting class. *Sunglasses off or on?*

She removed her sunglasses. "Sure thing."

"Look close, mind you." The policeman held out the picture of a dark-haired girl with good cheekbones, straight brows and bright eyes. Frankie had to look twice before she was certain it was her own photograph. Yes. It was the still shot the woman at the Central Casting wicket had taken of Frankie when she'd signed up to be an extra for two short days before.

"No, can't say that I have. What did she do?"

"Killed a movie star."

"Gilbert Howard? It was in the news, wasn't it?"

"Yep. And neither you nor the rest of the world has seen her." The policeman took back the photo, tucked it into his uniform pocket and rolled in his policeman's boots the way Frankie rolled in her brogues, back and forth, from heel to toe. "Well, it's the end of my shift and I've got sore feet."

Emboldened by success, Frankie nodded at the picture in his hand. "I bet she'd rather have sore feet than this manhunt."

The policeman chuckled. "Ain't that the truth, pal? But we'll catch her."

Frankie hid her anger. "What sort of evidence have you of her guilt, anyway? What if this woman Francesca—Frankie—Ray didn't kill Gilbert Howard at all?"

"She killed him. Sure as shootin'. Well, that's it—I'm gone for the day. Gilbert Howard will go unavenged on my shift." He patted the pocket with her photograph in it and turned away, speaking over his shoulder as he ambled away. "Dirty bastard Howard was, too—I shouldn't say, but we almost got him on indecency charges a few times."

Frankie said to the policeman's back, "So, Gilbert Howard gets a shrug for crime he did commit, but Francesca Ray gets the chair for a murder she didn't commit?"

The policeman's sore feet had already taken him off along Sunset Boulevard, and he didn't hear her. The light was fading fast, but a good percentage of the glamorous drivers who passed her by, were still wearing sunglasses, so with an unsteady hand she set her own dark glasses back on her nose.

Publicity had been clear that Frank Achilles must show up at Camillo's in good time, and about a few more things as well. Frankie hoped she remembered them all—how to make an entrance, and that her left profile was the better to present to the cameras. Or was it the right? Hurrying, she made her way along storefronts and past a small adobe church, to Camillo's.

Night fell in its swift California manner as she arrived at the entryway to the restaurant. Frankie paused under the striped awning, as Publicity had instructed her to do, to attend the starlet Billie Starr and Publicity's photographer. She chose to wait not too near the doorman. There was no need to court exposure.

The doorman held open the glass doors for a young couple. The man wore dinner whites, and the woman wore satin and a melting look, which she bestowed upon Frankie. She slung her spotted fur over her shoulder, the long end trailing after her like a faithful, fleshless pet. The doorman shut the door after the couple, but not before the heavy aromas of cherry pie and creamed chicken had slipped out the doorway and up inside Frankie's nose. Her stomach growled.

The doorman must have heard the rumble. "Are you going inside, sir?"

Frankie said, "My dinner companion is late arriving."

"The prettier they are, the later they arrive. Cigarette?" The doorman looked over his braided shoulder at the door and held out a pack, adding, "I wouldn't ask, but you seem a bit jittery. And it's night-time."

She frowned. "What about it?"

"It's night-time, and you're wearing dark glasses."

As Frankie removed the glasses, the doorman held out the cigarettes again. They were Camels, Frankie noted, refusing them with thanks. As if Connie were at her side, she heard her laugh, and the confident whisper: *What do you like in a smoke, Frankie?* Frankie always used to answer, *"Good health and long life, because doctors recommend Camels over any other cigarette."*

Frankie stepped out from under the restaurant awning and looked up at the sky. Stars came out no matter how many policemen were showing your picture around town. Even if the cops caught her, convicted her, and took her the short mile to the electric chair, the stars would keep coming out, one by one, each night.

Frankie said to the doorman, "I feel like a lemon drop Hollywood picked up, rolled around on its tongue a couple of times and then spat out into an ashtray."

"Sure you do." The doorman grinned around the butt end of his cigarette. "I was like you, pal, not so long ago. I *was* you, hoping I'd made it right out of the wrapping and into the movies. Never panned out. Now I just open and close the door here at Camillo's Fine Bar and Grille."

"Bad luck, I guess," Frankie said politely.

"Well, there are worse things than failure."

It occurred to Frankie that everybody who was anybody came to dine at Camillo's, and a doorman was a darned good source to ask about the night of the murder. "You got that right. Look at Gilbert Howard."

"Now there's a case in point. Howard was always here, dancing in patent leather shoes, dipping the girls over the bend in his arm. Now he's boxed up, nothing left but his movies, poor old chap." The doorman tapped the ash from his cigarette into the low box hedge by the door.

"I guess you've seen it all," Frankie said. Several more people passed by, and she recognized two of them from the movie magazines. She knew their names, and she knew their movie roles, but she found that just now she didn't much care. The time was right to ask the question.

She asked, "Was Gilbert Howard here two nights ago?"

"Sure he was. Poor old fellow. He was always kind to me."

"Who was he with?"

"Who wasn't he with? He was one of the fortunate few, all right. Here's what happens to most fellows in Hollywood. What happens is, at the start a young man like you who's new in town gets invited everywhere. Like I did. We're like male ballet dancers, you know? To hold up the ladies to view. You get the invite to Cukor's or Thalberg's and you play a couple dozen sets of tennis at Chaplin's, and then suddenly you're old hat. Some new face comes to take your place at the parties, with the ladies. Soon enough you realize they're just moving you along the conveyor belt and out the flap at the back. And then, at some time or other, a fellow's got to face facts." Gloved hand held out for his tip, the doorman let a slick fellow in perfect black tie pass on through. "Say, see that woman over the other side of the road, her in the leopard skin? I spooned with her once at a party beside a champagne fountain. Think she remembers? Nix. But I do. I remember everything. Say, cast your eyeballs at the Packard, chum."

Frankie nodded appreciatively at a large car as it slowly approached the awning. She tried again. "Last night, before he was murdered, was Howard here with a blonde girl? Slender, bobbed?"

But the doorman had lost interest in Frankie. The Packard pulled up to the curb. Under the streetlights it had appeared grey, but on closer inspection it proved to be a lustrous lavender shade. The strange paint job attracted a small crowd from up and down the sidewalk, to rubberneck at whatever famous person was inside.

The doorman pushed through the gogglers. Frankie moved after him. "I just want to know, can you remember whether Gilbert Howard at least danced with a blonde woman last night?"

"What? Sorry, I got to do the job." The doorman bent to open the Packard's door. Frankie and the crowd were treated to the sight of a silver lamé shoe, a perfect silken ankle, and a swath of pleated chiffon skirt the same platinum colour as Frankie's new froth of hair.

Billie Starr. A pale hand tipped in rose red nails extended itself to the doorman, who bent to help Frankie's date out of the Packard's shadowy interior.

"Watch the merchandise," the starlet called out to the driver. Startled, Frankie fumbled her dark glasses back on. She recognized the starlet's voice. It wasn't Billie Starr at all.

Connie Mooney climbed out of the Packard.

Frankie wished for a chair to sit down on. But she'd spent the day in character as Frank Achilles, and she was not about to abandon it now. She shot her cuffs and said, "Evening, Miss Mooney."

"Mr. Frank Achilles. Publicity told me you'd be waiting for me." Connie lowered her eyelids and exuded a peculiar well-rounded dignity that she'd employed to poleaxe males since her twelfth birthday. "Pleased to meet you. Look out, they're going to take the first shots."

On the far side of the Cadillac a man in a pinch-waist suit was climbing out. He hurried around the back end of the car, hefting a flash camera in one hand while he gestured with the other. "Right, children, stand together, suck in what stomach you can, and gimme some enthusiastic teeth."

Connie straightened up. "Like this?"

"Publicity said to shoot my left profile," Frankie told him.

The photographer said one of several words Frankie's father didn't know she knew. "Let a professional do the work, fella. And don't waste time." The photographer jerked his chin at the restaurant door. "I heard Garbo's on her way. First sighting since February."

"Greta Garbo is a quiet woman," the doorman interjected reminiscently. He moved to stand just outside camera range. "Sensitive about her long feet. I myself think they are perfectly in proportion."

Frankie and Connie stood side by side. The camera flashed. Frankie mumbled out of the side of her mouth, "Hey, where's Billie Starr? I promised to take her to dinner."

"You'll have to ask Publicity, Mr. Achilles. I'm just doing what I'm told." Connie was checking the hem of her skirt and didn't look up. The bulb flashed again, and again.

The photographer eyed the doorman, who had edged into the last shot. "Say, what's your game, buddy?"

"I just open the doors. You folks have a happy evening," the doorman said. To Frankie, he added, "In answer to your question, by the way, I guess Gilbert Howard was mostly with Marietta Valdes. Or, was that the night before?"

"Please, try to remember." Frankie held out her elbow to Connie.

"With fellows like Gilbert Howard, anything's possible," the doorman said. "There's an available blonde on every corner when you're that big in the films. But I thought he was dancing with Miss Valdes the night he died. Or maybe it was Ida Lupino. Or both of them."

Frankie was more disappointed in this answer than she would have believed possible.

"Mr. Achilles, you're a bit shaky," Connie muttered to Frankie. "Don't tell me you're as nervous as I am."

"I haven't eaten all day," Frankie told her. She took a breath and dived right in. With Connie, it was always the best way. "Look, don't react. It's me, Frankie."

Connie made a little noise and looked Frankie in the eye for the first time. "It's those darn sunglasses," she said. "Frankie! For the love of Michelangelo. Is dressing you up like a man Publicity's joke? Tonight wasn't supposed to be funny."

Frankie asked, "Where have you been? You should have left me a note to explain why you weren't coming home, at least. All kinds of things have happened. Haven't you read the news?"

"Not today." Connie said. "And there's no bigger news than this: I was with King Samson. Being groomed for tonight. I left you a message—the Lucky Strike cigarette pack. Cats, Frankie! If you didn't understand the message *Lucky Strike*, I despair of you."

"What's so important about tonight?" Frankie asked. "What's such a big deal that you couldn't at least telephone the Queen?"

"You are acting like my *mother*. I thought the whole idea was that we were going to try and be movie stars." Connie peered in through a side window into the restaurant through the bank of gardenias just inside the anteroom door. "It's all set up for tonight. I'm supposed to have my picture taken at Camillo's having dinner with a handsome actor. And then later on, something big—that photographer has no idea how big."

Something big? Gilbert Howard was dead. What was bigger than that? And how was it possible to be in Hollywood and not know that one of its greatest stars was dead?

A fellow in a dinner jacket stepped forward. He, too, flashed a camera at them. "Just the house photog, folks. But I guess you're used to it."

"Swell," Connie said to him. To Frankie she whispered, "We don't tip these photographers, do we?"

"I think that if you tried to tip that first fellow he'd black your eye for insolence. Listen, so much has happened that I don't even know where to begin." Should she start with the accusation of murder, or with the finding of the body? Or open with her disguise and work from there? What about Billie Starr, and the Queen? And Eugene Ellery, whose every move invited further questions?

But at the far end of the foyer the head waiter was holding the door open for them. So commanding was he that it seemed best after all to begin by taking Connie's elbow.

Tall mirrors on both sides showed the two of them stepping toward the dining room, into an eternity of reflected and diminishing distances. Ahead of them she made out a room panelled in dark wood, from which flowed the curlicues of piano music and a hum of conversation. Frankie snatched a glance at Connie's expertly painted face, recalling the time when they were six and wore Connie's mother's rouge to school and had their cheeks scrubbed nearly raw by the vice-principal.

Under her breath, she asked Connie, "Then haven't you heard about Gilbert Howard? He's dead."

"Not poor Howie?" Connie said. "That's terrible. Heart attack?"

"Somebody shot Gilbert Howard." Frankie stood up straight and took a step forward into the room. A waiter stood to each side, a little way behind, holding the doors wide, as one would hold back a stage curtain for the star to take a bow. Ahead of them at the bottom of the steps, glorious in black tails, stood the head waiter, waiting. And beyond him Frankie was aware, in a confused and distant sort of way, of mermaids and palm trees and an unexpectedly white piano. "The police think I murdered him. Smile," she said.

Chapter Four

To enter Camillo's dining room, you had to travel down a couple of steps.

Frankie remembered Publicity's directive to pause a moment at the top of the steps. Publicity had predicted that all eyes would turn their way, and he was right. Frankie surprised herself with a sudden desire to turn and run. However, curiosity steadied her, for half-dozen living mermaids, dressed in silken fishtails and beaded clamshells, posed about the room on raised boxes set against the walls. Round tables glittered with glassware and candles, and waiters crisscrossed the restaurant, balancing trays and dishes with chrome covers. The well-dressed clientele filled every table, adding a warm buzz of voices to the carelessly perfect vowels of a talented alto leaning against the piano. Trying not to rubberneck, but at the same time taking in every detail, Frankie followed Connie and the maitre d' across the room.

Connie hissed, "The police thought you did it? Listen, Frankie, this is no time to joke."

"No joke. Abso-tively true."

"Applesauce," Connie said, although there was a note of doubt in her voice.

"No ma'am. No apples anywhere, Newtown or Gravestein."

They settled at a central table for two. A busboy wove his way toward them through the mermaids and the diners, set a bucket of ice beside them on a chrome-plated stand, and moved off again. One of the mermaids near the white piano began combing her hair, which Frankie had always heard mermaids did, although she herself had been raised not to comb her hair in the dining room. "We're a long way from cantaloupe and ice cream at the Aristocrat Café."

"We're puttin' on the Ritz. Now, Frankie." Connie was suddenly serious. "Any fool would know that you didn't murder Howie."

"Of course not. But the foolish world thinks I did."

"No baloney?" Connie asked doubtfully.

"I'd be happy if it *was* baloney, but it's not. Check the papers, you'll see my picture reprinted from the shot they took of me at Central Casting."

"Phooey. Well, your disguise is good. We'll just have to wait for the silly world to catch on that you're innocent."

"The only problem with that—" Frankie began.

Connie waved all Frankie's problems away with her menu. "I can't get over your disguise. You look just like a very handsome man."

"It's acting, more than anything," Frankie pointed out. "You know my tenor voice I use in men's roles? But I must admit that the Queen of the Extras showed me how to walk like a man."

"She's an artist. By the way, the dinner tab's on the studio. We can order what we like." Connie peered around the side of her menu at Frankie. "Do you think we should order the Lobster Newburg or the New York Steak?"

A waiter advanced upon them, soft-footed. He suggested the Chicken Halibut.

"How can you have Chicken Halibut?" Connie demanded. "Mother Nature says it's got to be one or the other. Make up your mind, buddy."

Frankie smothered a smile as the waiter explained that Chicken Halibut was simply young halibut. "Like a chick is young, miss. And by good fortune we have just two servings left."

"You've got to be kidding. Halibut? You can stick that in your hat," Connie laughed. "Tell him what we want, Frankie. I mean, *Frank.*"

Frankie took a deep breath and ordered champagne. Connie ordered lobster for both of them.

Once the waiter had left, his disappointment in their choice nearly hidden behind a professional exterior—which was a sort of acting, too—Connie let out a huff. She rested her elbow on the table, chin on hand.

"You did *tell* them you didn't kill Gilbert Howard?"

"It's a long tale of bad luck and sorrow," Frankie said. "Let me tell you what happened."

"Just a minute, somebody's taking our picture over there. I should take up smoking. Look at the way it shows off a girl's manicure." A bulb flashed across the room, and Connie craned her neck around. "Now the photographers are taking pictures of the mermaids, though it won't help their acting careers much. Who looks at your bone structure when you're wearing a shell brassiere?"

The waiter reappeared and poured them two long-stemmed glasses of champagne.

Frankie said, "Blanche Carver accused me of killing Gilbert Howard. Wait! That house photog is just about to take our pictures again. Raise your glass."

"Link arms," Connie suggested, and they did, just before another flash went off. She added, "Oh, shoot! I wish you'd been a real movie star. It's hard to keep a straight face and act lovey-dovey when it's just you."

Frankie laughed out loud. Everything was different, now that she was no longer alone. Connie was stubborn, and she didn't always notice what words came out of her mouth, but when the chips were down she was true blue. Frankie's mood improved still further when she saw the waiter coming their way with a large platter balanced on his shoulder. He set before them two steaming dishes of lobster, with sauce thick with cream and as rich as seven bankers.

"Frankie, tell me everything while we eat."

Frankie began with her great moment as a pigeon girl, which it turned out Connie had missed, since King Samson had pulled her aside to talk to her about a screen test while Luigi was filming Frankie. Connie listened, satisfyingly wide-eyed, as Frankie related the finding of Gilbert Howard's body, her night in Eugene Ellery's cupboard, her transformation into Frank Achilles, and her subsequent pursuit of Billie Starr.

"Has the world gone crazy? There's not the slightest case against you," Connie said firmly. "*I* think the murderer was Marietta Valdes. She came by the studio in the afternoon, but she was off again by dinnertime."

"But Marietta is the last person in the world to wish Howard dead—he was *helping* her become a director, and about the only person willing to help a woman, too."

"Bushwah," Connie said. "Nobody could seriously suspect you, Frankie. You're safe as houses."

"Don't underestimate the police. There's a circumstantial case against me," Frankie pointed out. "And don't forget the power of the law to railroad a swift trial—"

"Don't worry about any of that nonsense," Connie interrupted. "You're innocent. Stay disguised until the thing all blows over. I bet they find the real killer by tomorrow. And listen, I was just kidding—I don't *really* mind that you're my escort for the evening."

"Thanks." Frankie frowned. Perhaps it was just as well that Connie appeared not to have a complete understanding of the danger of Frankie's circumstances. It might very well be that her nonchalance would serve them well. A panicky Connie at a roadblock or border would help neither of them when they made their escape.

Frankie held a sip of champagne in her mouth so that the bubbles pricked her tongue. She remembered the song they used to sing at Girl Guide camp when she and Connie were eleven. They sat side by side with arms folded on knees before the campfire, faces hot where the heat caught them, backs chilly where the warmth didn't reach, singing in the night. *Make new friends but keep the old, one is silver and the other is gold.* The sparks had sounded like firecrackers dancing up against a black sky. Next day, she and Connie had been sent home for sneaking out of camp for a midnight swim, but what stuck with her were their voices, uncertain in key, piping the roundelay.

You could accomplish anything with the help of a friend. You might even find a way out of town when the police were on your tail.

"Connie, I'm going to need your help."

"I'm going to need *yours*." Connie set her fork down on the plate.

Frankie said, "Tonight, the most important thing is to get back to Paradise Gardens and see whether Eugene managed to find the girl who was kissing Gilbert Howard beside the swimming pool."

"They're snapping our picture again. Lean in."

Champagne corks and flashbulbs popped around the dining room.

Connie said, "Look, we've talked about your situation. Now it's my turn."

"But—"

"No buts. I've got a big opportunity ahead of me tonight, with the burning of the *Ambition* set—"

"You don't understand the severity of my situation." Frankie took a deep breath. Connie hadn't seen Gilbert Howard's body.

She hadn't lived through the long dark hours lying hidden in Eugene Ellery's closet. No wonder the peril didn't seem real to her. "Just now, a policeman was showing around my picture. They have my name. It's just a matter of time—"

"No, *you* don't understand." Connie made the puffing sound she always made when her mother offered a suggestion she considered too misguided for human consideration. "Look, Frankie, I'm not going to let anything happen to you. We'll work through this together. We always have. A smart policeman will take over from the stupid ones and find Howie's killer—I still can't believe he's gone—and you'll be fine."

Frankie shook her head.

Connie ploughed onward. "Publicity's got a terrific photography shoot for us in a few minutes. And I've got an even better plan I thought up when King Samson mentioned that an army of engineers and firemen will burn down the big *Ambition* set at the studios tonight. Just keep your nerve, Frankie, and stay disguised as Frank Achilles, and everything will be all right."

Frankie said, "Connie Mooney, this is a matter of life and death. I didn't want to say so before, but if I don't solve Gilbert Howard's murder soon, somebody's going to recognize me. When they do, they'll call the police. Then the police will either throw me in jail, or they will shoot me trying to escape capture. Do you want that to happen?"

"Of course not." Connie leaned close. "But tonight is the night they'll film the *Ambition* set burning. It's the only night I can make my plan happen. After that, you can hide out in Paradise Gardens. You're one of the Queen's family, just like me. The kids won't turn you in."

"The police will search Paradise Gardens again. Do you want Tom and the Queen and the other kids charged with hiding an accused murderess? That's not like you, Connie."

But possibly, Frankie thought, it was. She remembered the many times she'd shut her ears to her father's diatribes against Connie, and even more frequent occasions when she'd stood up to him on the subject.

"Connie, listen—"

"*You* listen. I'm trying to tell you my plan for being noticed in the movies, and you keep changing the subject. Darn! Here comes another photographer. Get ready." Connie turned to greet the man with the camera.

The photographer raised his camera. "Let's have a smile for the folks in Peoria." The camera flashed. The smell of the burned-out flash hung in the air as the cameraman popped the bulb out of his camera and replaced it with another from a bulging pocket. "Thanks on behalf of *Movie Mirror*, Miss Mooney and Mr. Achilles."

When the photographer was at a safe distance, Frankie said, "You are threatening our life-long friendship, Connie."

"I don't believe that for a minute. You're the one that's acting selfish. This opportunity I thought up for the fire at Monument Studios isn't just for me, you know. The farther I get in the films, the more I can help you. That's how we planned it and that's how it's going to be."

Frankie shook her head, chewing away. "Right now lobster is the only thing I like about this conversation."

"Look, Frankie, the big fire later on tonight is really a complicated set-up. And as for what is going to happen right now and right here at Camillo's, it's that photo opportunity that Publicity thought up for us. I don't have time to explain, so follow my lead. *Act.* Here she comes."

Frankie turned — every head in the room turned — to see the doors open. A vision in red entered. Marietta Valdes posed at the top of the steps, overlooking the dining room of Camillo's.

Expectation ruled the moment. The room grew almost quiet as Marietta, gleaming, descended the steps to the floor. All eyes followed her.

But with a swish of red taffeta, Marietta sauntered past diners and photographers as if they were so many shell-bedecked mermaids. A little kerfuffle arose as the photographers picked up their cameras. Frankie noted that there was quite a bit of business necessary to work the flashes.

An elderly couple gaped across their champagne glasses as Marietta stopped at their table. She said, "A lot of people don't know this, but a director is not a craftsman. He is a magician, and story is transformation. May I?"

She took the elderly woman's upraised glass and drained it, then handed it back. "The publicity head doesn't understand dramatic tension. I would have set this scene up in the front lobby, I think, where one passes through a narrow casement. And I would film the shot from the right into the mirrors, bearing in mind the golden ratio, that rectangle beloved of the ancient Greeks." She turned to a solitary female diner nearby. "Don't you think, dear?"

The woman fingered her beads and said, "I never thought anything like that in my life, Miss Valdes."

Across from Frankie, Connie was slowly turning pink. She muttered, "Marietta ought to be over here, having her picture taken with me. With you and me. I should have known she would ruin things. She's corned to the eyeballs."

Frankie felt this was a fairly safe interpretation of the scene, but Marietta Valdes drunk was still more interesting than most people sober. In that way, Marietta was rather like Gilbert Howard.

Marietta asked the room at large, "Does anybody here believe that a woman can direct a major motion picture?"

The room fell silent. Frankie waited. Marietta's face paled as the silence lingered. When one of the mermaids let out a stifled giggle, Frankie could bear it no more. She rose to her feet.

Connie snatched at her sleeve, but Frankie pulled free. "*I* do. I believe you'd craft an excellent motion picture, were you to direct it, Miss Valdes."

Marietta Valdes turned to their table. "Mr. Frank Achilles, don't say *craft*. A director is not a craftsman. A director is a god."

Connie muttered, "For Pete's sake, this is all wrong. I'm going to have to get this whole scene back on track. Help me out, Frankie." She stood up at Frankie's side. "Are you looking for me, Miss Valdes?"

Marietta said tiredly, "Ah. The redhead."

"Jiminy, about time," Connie hissed to Frankie "Marietta and I worked through this yesterday afternoon. I should have known she'd forget her lines and ruin everything."

But Frankie knew that Marietta Valdes was a star because she didn't ruin anything. She improved it.

"You're supposed to say, *Young talent,*" Connie hissed to Marietta. "I'm much younger than you."

"Marietta's all of twenty-two," Frankie hissed at Connie.

"I'll say the lines. *Youth!*" Marietta snatched up Connie's glass of champagne and drained it. "*Nobody* takes my co-star."

She placed one strong hand at the base of Frankie's back, the other behind her puffball hair, and kissed Frankie on the lips.

Flashbulbs flared. Once she'd gotten over her natural surprise, Frankie decided that being kissed by a woman was almost like being kissed by a man you were not actually involved with, like when you played Spin the Bottle. However, there was a subtle difference, lying perhaps in the element of surprise and the transfer of lipstick.

Marietta let Frankie go.

One of the mermaids called out from beneath a potted palm, "Hey, photog, how about that new fella, Frank Achilles, kisses some of us mermaids? And you take the shot for free."

There was a scattering of applause, but the scene felt as if it was over and the tension resolved. Frankie sensed that the audience was losing interest. Certainly most of the diners at Camillo's would, like Frankie, be regular readers of *Movie Mirror* and other Hollywood publications. They would know that some little star-studded drama was often to be found on the menu.

Connie's face had changed colour again, to a deeper rose. "Sit down, *Frank Achilles.* You're making fools of us."

"Redhead, don't you know why you're here?" Marietta sat herself down on the edge of Frankie and Connie's table. "This scene is not about raising you to my level, it's about making me look down into the abyss where you dwell." She took Frankie's glass and poured the last of the champagne into it.

Connie hissed, "What do you mean, *abyss?*"

Frankie said, "She means that King Samson set you up as a scare tactic to stop the real movie star, Marietta, from asking for more power than Samson wants to give. It's just like the audition in Vancouver."

"Is that so? Well, you don't know anything about anything, Frankie. *Frank.*"

Raising her glass, Marietta said, "Here's to you, Frank Achilles. You're going to make a very good movie star, if I have anything to say about it."

Frankie said, "Miss Valdes, for a lot of reasons I'm afraid that Frank Achilles is never going to be a movie star."

"Acting hard to get?" Marietta nodded. "That's the way to play the game."

Frankie clearly had the star's attention and goodwill. There would never be a better time to question Marietta Valdes about Gilbert Howard's murder. "I need to ask you something, Miss Valdes. When Gilbert Howard left you here at Camillo's two nights ago, where was he going?"

"I don't know," Marietta poured champagne into Frankie's glass, raised it in a toast, and drank. "Bless Howie for a free spirit."

"Didn't he say anything at all? It's really important."

"If it's so important, you should ask the right question. He didn't say *where*, but he did say *whom* he was going to. Into his true love's arms. Some unlucky woman. Howie was a great actor, and he believed I could direct, but he never saw the point in being faithful to one woman."

"And that's all he said? That he was going to see his own true love?"

"That's all." Marietta glanced at Connie. "I suppose I *should* apologize to the redhead here for veering off the script. Sorry, dearie. It was your big moment and I spoiled it, didn't I? Aren't stars *terrible*?"

Connie said, "This dinner was supposed to be a big dramatic scene for me. I was going to be in the papers."

Marietta beamed. "Serves you right, redhead. This was supposed to be my sister Billie's evening. Publicity promised to send Billie to dinner with Frank Achilles here, tonight. But Sammy must have told him to change the schedule."

"No wonder King Samson doesn't love you anymore," Connie said fiercely. "You'd better watch out, Marietta Valdes. You might already be a has-been and you don't even know it."

And there in the middle of Camillo's dining room, Frankie learned something about herself. She felt the clarity as an almost physical blow, midsection. Always, since her earliest recollected years, she had imagined that she was like her mother, optimistic and longing for an independent life. But now she felt the unhappy spirit of her father, the once Reverend Sheridan D. Ray, rise to its feet. Her anger expanded under its black surplice. She felt the colour rise in her cheeks and the bile in her belly. She stormed up to some imagined pulpit inside herself, growing larger with each step. She placed a hand on each side of the lectern, leaned out and passed a roaring internal judgment on Hollywood, its heartless and unintelligent police force, its malicious columnists and cruel producers, and on Connie herself, who she saw at last through her father's eyes.

She said, "You keep your mouth shut unless it's to apologize to Miss Valdes, Connie Mooney."

Rarely did Connie turn camellia white. There had been the long-ago instance when she'd punched a fellow who'd put his hand somewhere he ought not to have. And the last time she'd turned so pale had been during her screen test at the Dominion Theatre. But she'd never in her life looked at Frankie that way. A whole lifetime's friendship appeared to have boiled down to this one moment.

Connie said, "I hate you, *Frank Achilles*."

Frankie shot her cuffs. "*I* don't even like you that much." Frankie felt as cold as Lake Louise in December. She turned her back on Connie.

Without pause or regret she exited Camillo's dining room through the door the waiters used. It led through the kitchen, where dark eyes and Spanish voices cut through the steam. Now the tears fought their way into her eyes, so that she bumped into a fellow in whites. He swore as a platter of cutlets fell to the floor.

Frankie strode past him, past the ranges and the ovens, through a vast pantry and out into the alleyway, smelling of cats and greens past their prime. Careful of her brogues, she stepped around a slick of black oil Once out of the alleyway, she found herself on a much quieter Sunset Boulevard — the evening Sunset. She turned east toward the movie theatre near where she'd left the Model A.

A young man, dark as night, walked out from under the movie theatre marquee into the centre of Sunset Boulevard, plunked a bag down on the blacktop, and pulled out a trumpet. Frankie stopped in her tracks and stared.

Without a glance at the cars that blew past on either side, he raised the trumpet to his mouth, puffed his cheeks like a bullfrog, and blew the first long brassy note up at the sky, so that the note swept the heavens like one of the searchlights above Hollywood. On the far side of the street the marquee lit him from behind and cast a long black shadow across the road. And still the note went on and on, as his bullfrog neck puffed out and sweat beaded the hills and planes of his face. Frankie stood astonished by the glory of it, while he pulled that silken sound out of his yellow trumpet like a magician hauled an endless flow of scarves from his sleeve.

He stopped eventually, of course. He had to snatch his bag up in time to step out of the way of an oversized produce van. He saluted it cheerfully with his instrument, and Frankie fell in love with the young trumpet player, just as she'd fallen in love with Gilbert Howard and his irresistible talent.

She raised a hand to the musician and called out, "What's the name of that song?"

He crossed to Frankie's side of the street. "The Jailhouse Blues."

How appropriate. She closed her eyes for a moment and pictured herself in jail, all in grey, with her tin cup and tray. And that was better than imagining herself in the so-called Hot Seat at the moment when the warden's hand reached for the big U-shaped power switch.

Startled by the silence, she opened her eyes to see the musician watching her, polishing the mouthpiece with the cuff of his suit jacket.

"Do you know 'Dora Heart'?" she asked him.

"I know everything. But I'm sick and tired of blowin' 'Dora Heart.'"

She nodded. "I'm alone and a complete failure. Do you think I should go home to Vancouver?"

"Who'd have thought it, a white fellow in a good suit giving up?" The trumpet player laughed. "And I got picked to play a scene in the movies today, me and my trumpet. Ain't it funny?"

"I'm glad for you." She wished she were not so bone-deep tired.

And, if wishes came true, she'd stand there and listen to this fellow play forever. But the police were still after her.

She urged him, "Blow, brother, blow!"

"That's all I do, buddy." He grinned around his mouthpiece, threw back his head, and blew.

Frankie tore off to the car.

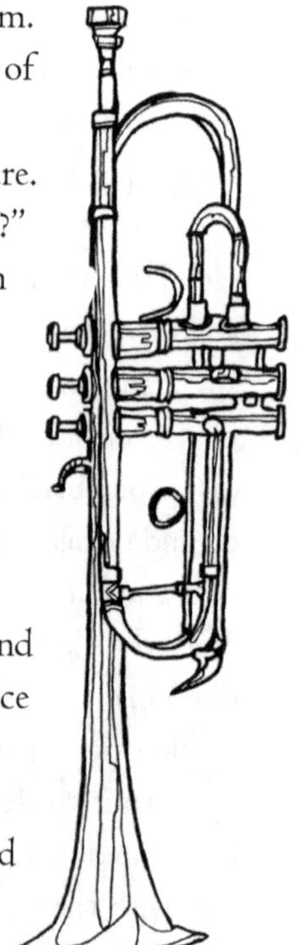

WINTER'S FLOWER

KT Wagner

KT Wagner *writes speculative fiction in the garden of her home on the west coast of Canada. She loves to knit and is a collector of strange plants, weird trivia, and obscure tomes. KT graduated from Simon Fraser University's Writer's Studio in 2015. She organizes writers' events, and works to create literary community, though much of this effort has been temporarily derailed by the pandemic. KT can be found online at northernlightsgothic.com and @KT_Wagner.*

Winter's Flower

The late September sun warms Gerda's arthritic knees while sparrows chirp from the roof. Her knitting needles slide and click, keeping rhythm with the squeak of her rocking chair against the porch floor. Across each row, she knits in the present, then purls back in her memories.

She learned to purl after Nan died, and every day since, Gerda remembers Kay.

Today, her daydream is about their childhood garden in the garrets and gutters of a faraway town.

Her hands turn the row, and the sweet scent of fall roses wafts by.

She brings the yarn to the front and remembers the roses of her childhood. They flourished in wooden rooftop boxes.

"We're happier here, planted in the ground," the present-day roses sing when she knits a row.

Gerda lives on the other side of the world from where she lost Kay so long ago. Now she knits her memories of the boy she loved into every garment she makes. The elaborate lace patterns were impossible in garter stitch. They require the memory purls.

Initially, the memory of grief drowned her, but she now knows Kay's still alive. The flowers told her.

Gerda loops yarn around the needle, drops a stitch, then purls three together.

More than sixty years have passed since the old woman, Nan, moved Gerda and the entire house to southern British Columbia. Gerda still marvels over that magical feat. She held Nan in awe for so long and still misses her despite everything.

In Denmark, gawkers, and others who'd read the story, disturbed them constantly. Some accused Nan of terrible things and tried to lure Gerda away. The endless need to protect their privacy had taxed Nan's magic.

This location is home now, reasonably far north but outside of the Snow Queen's range.

Gerda's been around magic most of her life and always longed for some of her own.

"There's nothing you can do, child." Nan had sympathized. "Perhaps that's why the river brought you to me."

Nan has since passed to the realm of the moon and stars, but some of the old woman's earthly magic persists.

For so long, Gerda believed Kay and the Snow Queen only existed within the story. She'd wondered aloud at the intensity of her love for the boy, a character in a fiction.

Nan had explained while she taught Gerda to knit, "Your deep attachment to the little boy proves the story is powerful and timeless." Heat from Nan's gnarled, guiding hands radiated into Gerda's small fingers as she struggled to manipulate the wooden needles.

The warmth of the memory is tinged by the ice-coated realization of betrayal Gerda works hard to ignore. The cold has seeped across the back of her neck, and she shivers and reaches for a shawl. The ache inside her festers. Grief and loss dig a pit, and soon, Gerda fears, she'll unravel into it.

Occasionally, the flowers relay a sighting of Kay, but it's proven impossible to make sense of their tales.

"Our fireweed cousins glimpsed Kay. He carried a nectar-scented basket," the evening primroses sang. When pressed for details, they recited a ditty about fields of cottongrass swaying in the wind.

"Alpine milkvetch tells stories of an ice maiden accompanied by a little boy with blue skin and hoar-frost hair." The sweet peas giggled. "But we don't know exactly when or where. Want to hear about our cousin who grew tall enough to touch the clouds and turned into a ladder?"

Gerda declined. She'd heard that story many times.

The flowers worry about their southern cousins and brethren. "They're easily burned by the expanding frost," they lament in unison, the air sugar-scented by their distress. "Poor hollies, magnolias, and camellias. There's no time to adapt to the changes. Their strength is being sapped."

"It will get better," Gerda keeps assuring them. It's a hope, not a lie. Gerda tries to coax the flowers to search for Kay, but they have their own priorities.

The winters are too cold and the summers too hot, they complain.

Time runs differently here than in the outside world. Gerda wonders if the same is true of the Snow Queen's lair. As a young woman, she trekked there once but, contrary to rumour, didn't find Kay, only signs he might have been there. A sliver of dark mirror, a small sled, and a pair of red shoes she couldn't quite place but knew were significant.

A river of winter blues flows from Gerda's needles. She's crafting a blanket for the cold days ahead. She carefully sets the project aside and stands. The rocker continues to rock. A list of chores demands attention, but first she'll visit Nan. The old woman is buried at the edge of the orchard, beneath an apple tree just outside the fenced and warded boundaries of the house and the rose garden. While there, Gerda will pick a basket of ripe fruit.

"I like the idea of fully returning to the earth," Nan explained when Gerda objected to her requested grave site. "Within the house grounds, the magic will preserve my body. It won't want to let me go."

Gerda didn't want to let her go either, but the end came, and she buried her long-time companion according to her wishes.

She shuffles down the porch stairs and is halfway across the yard before her joints warm up and she can walk with relative ease. She's accepting of the slow pace. It's an opportunity to admire the flowers and say good morning.

Ice trickles down her spine, and a sudden tension pulls her toward the gate. She clutches the empty basket. Nan is gone, but sometimes it feels like she calls to Gerda. Of course, it's her imagination. Loneliness has her believing in ghosts. At least ghosts might be able to answer her questions.

On the other side of the fence, a tarnished-silver sky glows. A chill wind curls around Gerda's ankles. Perhaps she should have worn a hat and mittens.

The apple tree is coated in ice, the fruit gone. Only apple-shaped ice hangs from the branches. Ghost apples. The syrupy stench of rotted fruit lingers.

Icy fingers of magic skitter across Gerda's face and hands. Her heart swells in alarm. It's too early and too far south, but there's no doubt. The Snow Queen was here. The world is changing, and not for the better.

Snowflakes swirl around the apple tree. Gerda reaches for one, and it stings her finger. A drop of dark-red blood wells and melts the sliver of ice. A snow bee careens toward the ground and disappears into the slush.

The chill tightens its grip on her. She hasn't seen a snow bee since before she came to live with Nan. The shawl isn't large enough to protect her.

Gerda closes her eyes and concentrates. She senses Kay's presence, distant but clear. Magic must be taking up residence inside her, but is it hers or Nan's? If only she could discuss this with Nan. Gerda sighs. If only she could trust everything Nan had told her.

Kay places four empty honey-collecting jars in each of two baskets. He wove them from arctic grasses—a couple of the endless tasks the ice maiden has set for him. He hardly thinks about the routine; it's what he does, and has done, for as long as he can remember.

The ice maiden requires the honey. It nourishes her power and her blood, warming it enough that it flows freely through her frozen veins. Her blood nourishes Kay.

The snow bees dislike him and are normally only active at night; but, like everything else, that seems to be changing.

With winter solstice less than three months away, the hours of daylight shrink. Soon it'll be dark almost all the time and he'll have to move fast to gather even a little honey.

She used to store honey for the winter months, but she's grown erratic and needy, consuming everything he gathers with no care for the future.

Once, Kay tasted the honey. It scorched his throat and he vomited and fell ill. She was very angry and locked him in a cave for days with only ice to eat. He shudders and pushes the memory aside. Best not to think about it.

Days, weeks, months, and years run into each other. Nothing much changes. Not him or his surroundings. How much time has passed? He has no idea. There is nothing before or after this life.

He wanders down the steps of the ice palace and trudges across the tundra. The bees built their hives in the permafrost, forming large, pingo-like domes.

A white cloud churns along the horizon. Uninterested, he notes it only because the ice maiden demands he report everything out of the ordinary.

Last week, a patch of blooming purple saxifrage poked through the snow and said hello before asking after the ice maiden. He hasn't seen purple saxifrage this far north in decades. Upon hearing about the flower's inquiry, the ice maiden stirred up storms for two days.

The sun warms his head and hands. He'll try harder not to notice anything. It would be easier if he could keep his eyes closed.

A low ridge defines the western edge of the honey fields. Kay crests it and stops. His frozen heart pumps syrupy blood through his veins. He drops the baskets. The hives have collapsed. The snow bees are swarming.

Long-dormant brain cells spark to life. "Run, Kay," they scream. "Now, she'll have no use for you."

He has ignored these voices before, but this time a faraway, yearning call lends strength to their message.

Kay doesn't think. He turns south, and runs.

Back inside the grounds of her house, Gerda leans on her walking stick and tries to calm her breathing. Modern transportation is too risky. To know which way to go, she must remain connected with the earth. She'll need a pack, sturdy walking shoes, Nan's walking stick, some food, and a camp roll for sleeping.

Pink flowers jut from a clump of mossy rockfoil. They call to Gerda. "Our cousins, the purple saxifrage, send warning — the snow queen is confused and erratic. Her kingdom melts, and they fear it's driven her insane. She's stirring up a polar vortex. The honey boy has fled."

"Kay?" Gerda asks, and her heart answers.

The wide world proves too much for Gerda. Icy winds howl, snow-that-should-be-rain clogs swaths of burnt forest. She leans into the walking stick. Everything has changed from what she remembers.

For days she continues to try, stopping only to knit and gather her bearings, but the land and the elements block her. She can neither go on nor back. Her heart is heavy in her chest.

In this moment, the buzz of bees catches her attention. She almost misses the blue-skinned boy running on top of the snow. His bare feet throw an ice spray in his wake, holding back the swarm.

The bees chase the child. They'll catch him if he falters.

Gerda points Nan's walking stick and charges toward the boy. She stumbles through the snow banks and ploughs on. It's no longer possible to know where the walking stick ends and her arm begins.

She must save the child. It no longer matters if he's Kay. She will not get to him in time, no matter how hard she tries.

"Child, I can help," she cries. "Get behind me."

He looks toward her with frost-clouded eyes and hesitates.

The bees engulf him.

Gerda screams, louder and longer than she's ever screamed before.

Her magic responds.

The swarm scatters, rises, reforms, and swoops away.

The child approaches. She wraps an arm around his shoulders and pulls him close. The hoar frost in his hair melts and runs in rivulets down his face. She recognizes Kay.

"I'm Gerda," she whispers. "I knew you were real."

He tilts his little face upward and scrunches his forehead. "I don't ..." A pause. "Grandmother?"

For a long moment, Gerda stares at her gnarled hand where it rests on Kay's narrow shoulder.

"Yes," she murmurs. "Grandmother. Come, child. I'll take you to the house. We'll eat last year's apples and talk to the flowers. We'll be safe there."

"I'm cold," he says.

She wraps her arms around him and hugs. "I'll knit you a sweater."

KALALOCH BEACH, WA
Michael Penny

Michael Penny has published five books, most recently Outside, Inside (McGill-Queen's University Press, 2014.) He lives on Bowen Island.

Kalaloch Beach, WA

When I first saw it at a distance
it was rock or over-sized drift-log.

The seagulls were also intrigued.
As I walked closer, the exposed jawbone

told me what it was and the wind stank solid
of salt and weeks-old meat.

It was a juvenile whale, a grey
and had beached on Independence Day.

Two weeks had split the skin and the intestines,
life's plumbing, spilled pillowy as dark clouds.

Its tail and fins were ragged stumps
with no reason to swim.

The split skin had reddened with sun and decay
and everything was so very still.

Until the seagulls squawked;
I was interrupting a peckable buffet,

and life did have to get on.
It was hard to walk away.

When a body's no longer needed
by its departed owner

what death leaves behind
remains for us a compelling display.

SYNCHRONICITY AND SONATA

Brandon Crilly

An Ottawa teacher by day, **Brandon Crilly** has been previously published by Daily Science Fiction, Abyss & Apex, OnSpec, Flame Tree Publishing, and other markets. He also reviews fiction for BlackGate.com and serves as a programming lead for Can*Con in Ottawa. With Evan May, he's the co-host of the podcast Broadcasts from the Wasteland, described as 'eavesdropping on a bunch of writers at the hotel bar'. You can find Brandon at brandoncrilly.wordpress.com or on Twitter @B_Crilly.

Synchronicity and Sonata

Over the sound of machinery, Eloise could almost drown out
Bariq's voice behind her. It didn't matter that she had known
Bariq for decades, that she celebrated Eid with his family every
year and had gone to him more than once for comfort during
Rebecca's worst days. Today it was like when she used to work
the floor; Bariq was just a suit trying to get in her way.

"Eloise, you know better than anyone that protocol—"

Three steps above him, she turned and glared. "And who
wrote that protocol?"

Bariq paused with both hands on the stair's railings; she saw
the admission in his eyes, but the fact that he wouldn't even say
the name *Rebecca* further churned the anger in her belly. Behind
him, the young foreperson—Eloise hadn't bothered to get her
name—wrung her hands, trusting Bariq to handle the situation
but still feeling the need to follow along. Apparently, she didn't
think she needed to be in the control room.

With the Core, this place will truly run itself, the board of directors had
championed. She always thought Rebecca insisted on working
with the board and staying on as foreperson because she didn't
trust the new system. Or maybe she had just been a creature

of habit. After this week, Eloise doubted how much she had known her wife.

"I've been a company shareholder for longer than you've worked here, Bariq. Shareholders' agreement says I have a right to inspect my investment."

"With proper notice. Not to mention proper attire."

Eloise tapped the hardhat she had grabbed below. Bariq looked pointedly at her black dress and high-heeled shoes, the latter still muddy from the funeral.

"If you care that much, call security." Before Bariq could plead some more, she said, "I just need to look."

"But the Core doesn't—" The foreperson dutifully stared at her boots the moment Eloise's glare shifted.

Bariq's expression softened, reminding her so much of everyone else at the funeral that she felt an old desire to find a tool and smack it against something, just to vent. Her years working the floor had made a mark on her beyond the physical one she still felt when she flexed her right hand. That surprised her, since her coding work had helped eliminate most of the jobs her friends and colleagues had cherished.

To help them find safer work. Better work, she'd told herself at the time. Entering the factory now, she felt like an unwitting accomplice in a fate she would never have chosen.

"You don't really think you'll find her out there, do you?" Bariq asked.

I did before, Eloise thought, remembering herself as a bright-eyed technician, butting heads with the veteran who was supposed to help her upgrade the entire floor. Her mind flashed through the tenuous months of getting to know Rebecca better, discovering the passion for her work that made her so stubborn, and everything that came after.

Eloise stepped out onto the catwalk and stared at the factory floor below. She had rarely come back here after she retired, and not once since Rebecca fell ill; the machinery looked nothing like what she coded for during most of her career. The robotic arms swinging over the parallel assembly lines were sleek and shiny, each one carefully cleaned and maintained during periodic shutdowns. The noise was nowhere near the cacophony that had required ear protection back in the day, and the cars being manufactured were different, too, thanks to the dramatic push away from fossil fuels. The space even smelled different. Beyond the expected lack of fumes and grease, the air was almost too neutral, but that might have been her mind playing tricks on her.

Her right hand squeaked as she clenched it around the catwalk railing; the joints in her fingers needed adjusting again. Rebecca was the reason Eloise became comfortable with the prosthetic. Even lying in a hospital bed, drained to exhaustion from experimental treatments, her wife asked about the hand and everything at home. That had been their promise to each other: to always keep on each other's toes.

Except Rebecca decided to leave. The note explaining why hadn't been enough. *I've been thinking about this for a while,* it said. *I'll be fine in there. It's where I belong. Go back sometime, okay? To remember the good times.*

That morning, as condolence after condolence rolled over her in time with the rain sluicing off her umbrella, as friends and loved ones remarked on how inspiring Eloise and Rebecca's marriage had been, Eloise thought: *How is someone giving up and running away inspiring?* While everyone else enjoyed tiny sandwiches at the funeral hall, Eloise hoped they wouldn't notice her running, too.

Only Bariq had. He leaned on the railing beside her. "Have you ever tried to hear it?"

"Hear what?" Eloise asked, with the same bitterness as if she'd said, "Fuck off."

"The tune."

"No."

If Bariq realized the lie, he didn't show it. It had taken her a while to see the machines as more than just hunks of metal with instructions for how to move, to realize what Rebecca meant when she said the factory *created its own tune*. She compared the synchronicity to an orchestra's movements; each machine was an instrument, and the foreperson was the conductor. If you closed your eyes and listened, Rebecca said, you could almost hear the tempo—but only the people who gave themselves to the Core understood it.

Malion Manufacturing prided itself on efficiency and well-designed technology, et cetera and so on, but no amount of automation could make a factory perfect. Machines developed unique imperfections as components were stressed, and a single kink anywhere on the line made the entire operation less effective, until it became so serious that it needed repairing. The Core was supposed to be a way to curb that. By adding human consciousness into the factory's network, the board argued, the machines could manage themselves with the intuition and teamwork humanity had developed through evolution.

Everyone who examined the coding—Eloise included—agreed that the research was sound. Early assessments seemed to indicate increased efficiency and decreased repair costs. And with the payout Malion offered, there were enough desperate or sick employees willing to sell their consciousness and provide for their loved ones.

But no one could adequately explain exactly what happened to people when their consciousness entered the Core, or how much of their individuality remained among the 'collective human mind', held within an artificial network. Eloise had been one of the last experts to sign off on the plan, and only after Rebecca gave her blessing to the review process for Core volunteers.

One of the machine arms near the front of the line, working on the chassis, caught Eloise's attention. She watched as it paused in place then leaned forward to weld the strut being held out by the arm before it. Another strut followed, and again the welder paused before completing its task. None of the other welders hesitated in the same way.

"Ever think that's why Rebecca passed on early retirement?" Bariq asked. "I always figured it was sheer stubbornness …"

"Do you see that?" Eloise asked, pointing not at the welder but at the arm beside it holding the strut. "That machine arm is leaning a little further than the others."

Bariq shook his head.

"Not every time, it—Look, there!" When he still didn't see it, she explained, "It isn't leaning the same way each time. Some internal mechanism. The welder is pausing for about a half-second each time so that it doesn't miss the spot it's supposed to hit."

The foreperson chimed in, "That's the point of the Core. Human ingenuity and—"

Eloise ignored her and started across the catwalk again. She studied the floor as she walked, examining each machine. Behind her, Bariq rambled about how that welder's behaviour was just an example of the Core at work, the collective being more intuitive with each person who uploaded. She shut him out again, not wanting to hear the corporate bullshit. None of that had ever mattered to Rebecca, and it certainly didn't matter to her.

She stopped at the other end of the catwalk. Ahead of her, a large loading crane loomed over the floor. When a completed car reached the end of its line, one of the crane's clawed appendages lifted it onto a conveyor belt that ferried it across to another factory for interior assembly and quality control. As the crane rotated toward the factory floor again, its appendages seemed to sway back and forth, its shadow moving across the smaller machines in front of it.

The bubbling anger in Eloise's stomach stilled. Her hand squeaked loudly as she grabbed the railing, and her legs started to shake. Bariq held a steadying hand near her shoulder as she slowly sank to her knees.

She watched as that massive crane plucked the next completed car from the assembly lines. Its claws swayed a little differently this time as it moved back into position.

"Just like a conductor," Eloise murmured.

For a week, she had imagined everything she wanted to say to Rebecca. That she didn't want the payment from Malion. That she didn't want Rebecca to give up and let her illness win. That if the love of her life thought she was sparing Eloise the pain of watching her decline, their marriage was nothing more than a God-damned cliché. Eloise just wanted her wife, for as long as she could have her.

Every angry and grief-stricken thought melted away as she watched the loading crane sway over the factory floor, gesturing to a different section of the line each time, cueing a different part of the orchestra. Almost the way Rebecca had saluted the floor with her coffee cup each morning and waved at it from the control room before she left.

It's where I belong. Go back there sometime, okay? To remember the good times.

Eloise closed her eyes and listened for the synchronicity. She couldn't hear it the way Rebecca could, but she thought she was closer than before.

She waved off Bariq's help as she got back to her feet. He seemed confused by her smile but didn't ask her to explain as she led him away.

Eloise paused about halfway down the catwalk to look back. She watched Rebecca's machine sway one more time, like a parting wave, and wondered why she ever thought her beloved had given up.

THE HUNTER UNDEAD

Erin K Wagner

Erin K Wagner grew up in southeast Ohio, on the border of Appalachia, but now lives in central New York, where she hikes in the Catskills and listens for ghostly games of ninepins. She holds her PhD in medieval literature and teaches literature and writing in the SUNY system. Her stories have appeared in a variety of publications, from Apex to Clarkesworld, and her second novella, An Unnatural Life, has just been released from Tor.com. You can visit her website at erinkwagner.com.

The Hunter Undead

I was not a man, and it was man's work to hunt the puffins on Drangey Island. Nonetheless, I was Briet Jakopsdóttir, and the other men knew and loved Jakop in their own fashion. Jakop was ill, and I had been to the doctor with him. He seemed small on the examination table, his stomach concave and his back bowed. The skin of his torso was white where it had never been exposed to the ocean winds. He had folded his yellowed undershirt and his cable sweater carefully and set them on the chair. The doctor was a long time in coming, and he held his hands, chapped, nails cracked, in his lap, uncomfortable while he waited.

"Tell the story, Faðir," I said, thinking the old pattern of the words might relax him. He had been the one to tell the tourists who visited the island the story of Grettir the Strong, the outlaw who had lived there in his exile some thousand years ago.

He shook his head. "Bad luck here," he said.

So in Jakop's absence, the men suffered me to come along. It was their way of saying to my father *get better* because a girl could not work with them for long. But they had not seen him, suddenly ancient. They had a way of avoiding the street and the house, a way of avoiding Sauðárkrókur during the spring hunting season. My father sat often in the window of the upstairs bedroom and looked out over the white-roofed houses to the slate waters of Skagafjorður and the square bulk of Drangey. We say that Drangey's two rocky outcroppings from the sea are the figures of a she-troll and her cow, turned to stone on the sun's rising. There was once a he-troll as well, but it has collapsed under the ocean and disappeared.

I drove every day, early in the morning and late in the twilight, back and forth between Sauðárkrókur and the coastal farm from which the boats left. I didn't steer the boat on which I rode but sat on the piles of net used for hunting. The other hunters, dressed in jumpers and overalls, stood around me, rocking with the movement of the boat. Wind and water splashed up, cold and arctic, and glistened on my jacket. I watched the rocky cliff of the island draw closer. We circled around the outcropping, the she-troll. Its surface was white with guano. The birds flew up in spirals, mirroring the backwash of the boat. They were black and white and orange. It seemed a shame almost to catch them, to stop their flight.

This early in the season, when the temperature was still cold enough to warrant thick gloves, there were fewer tourists. When they did come, they camped in old trucks and pop-up trailers around the farm. They drove into Sauðárkrókur for liquorice or a hot dinner, most likely puffin or lamb, with skyr as well. It was odd to have them on the boats, their necks craning for a better look at the island as we drew closer. For some, Drangey was the site of their own history, the place where Grettir died; for others—Americans and Europeans—it was both legend and exotic occupation at once. The island is not very accessible. It is nothing more than a cliff upon which we've staked out a narrow, crawling path. The Uppganga is steep, forty feet high, and we have to watch out for the tourists, make sure that they hold tightly to the ropes we've strung. For the birds, it is a different matter.

Jakop told the story of Grettir in his own way, stooping, standing, bending as the saga moved him. He always grew very quiet at the end when he told the tourists of Grettir's death, killed due to his rash assault on a piece of driftwood cursed by a witch. The axe he used slipped and bit deep into his own leg, and that wound was his undoing. The driftwood had seemed an innocent enough thing, tickling the black sand and rocks of the cove. I thought of it when we landed in the morning, the white sun cool and bright in the sky. Our boots rasped among the stones as we loaded the nets over our shoulders and moved to the Uppganga. I climbed up last so as not to hold up the others. I could feel them watching me and judging my pace.

They glanced at me also when I cast out the nets, drew the birds in, and snapped their necks. The birds lay in piles across the top of Drangey, marking our progress, feathers and blood ruffled by the winds. It was odd to hear the noise of the birds still living, too numerous to count and raucously loud, when looking out over the grass and seeing those still mounds. Their necks were thick, but fragile, in my hands. To wring their necks was the work of a moment because the puffins did not fear us. It was this the men liked to say was not the work of women. This, and the climbing, the staring down some fifty or sixty feet to freezing ocean. We were only twenty miles or so below the Arctic Circle. Or perhaps it was none of these things specifically. It may be they missed Jakop. I missed him, and I saw him each evening.

In our sagas, blood called for blood. A death did not go unanswered. But it also seemed like few men died of old age. Grettir did not struggle silently in an upstairs window against an encroaching tumour. Njal did not move listlessly from bed to table and stare at the canned soup bubbling in the pot. Maybe Egil, but he walked off the pages of his own story, refusing to die where we could see. Jakop had no such luxury. He refused to dress in anything more than his undershirt and woollen underpants. His arms were thin and knobby, speckled here and there with sun spots or rough patches of skin that did not go away. I sat across the table from him in the morning and could not eat my cereal. He looked up one morning, glancing out the window, though the gauze of the curtain hid most of the street. The sky was grey and red with dawn.

"Grettir killed the undead Glam at the end of the night, in the early morning like this," he said. "That is what I have always thought."

The shadows from the light made his face look thinner and sharper. Even Glam had carried more weight and substance on him. I pushed his bowl nearer him and had no patience for stories.

"Eat, Pabbi."

I turned away and did not watch him, shoving on my jacket. It was cold outside. The Corolla almost stalled out, but the engine finally turned over, and I backed out onto the street. I passed a delivery truck on its way into town, but no one else.

"We've got tourists today," Mikkel said to me offhandedly when I put the car into park beside the sod-roofed houses. He spoke through the window I had rolled down to hear the ocean as I drew close.

"Já," I said. The fact didn't seem particularly noteworthy.

"A shitload of them," he said. "We'll need to run a couple tours. I'm going to run you and the rest over with one load and then circle back for the others. Kit up."

I pulled the thick collar of my sweater high up over my jacket and zipped my jacket up to my chin. Then I yanked the hood down low. Amidst the green tufts of grass, there were horses and sheep. Dotted along the shore were also the tents and campers. Smoke drifted up from a campfire. I could hear the tourists on the shore, squawking like the birds in a mixture of Icelandic and English.

I helped the men load the nets, still heavy and damp from yesterday and from the night dew, onto the boat. Some threads were brown with old blood. The grey of dawn had never really gone, and now, in the full-fledged morning, the sky was overcast. Huddling in family and friend groups, the tourists boarded, crowded close to the deck railings. Mikkel revved the boat's engine and it lurched beneath us. The waves were choppy starting out. Fog was still thick in the air, and the further we drew away from shore, the thicker and whiter it seemed, taking over the dull sky. The bulk of the she-troll seemed only a shadow, frail and spectral, as we neared her and whipped around towards the cove on the island proper.

In the shadow of Drangey's cliffs, the cove felt dark and shut in. The screeches of the birds echoed and rebounded off the rocks. "Is it safe?" one of the tourists asked, and Mikkel had drawn aside with the other hunters, Runi, Pedró, and Sveinn, to discuss the same question.

"Up, up," Runi shouted, smiling, as the hunters broke apart. Mikkel was heading back to the boat. "We'll stay in front and in back of you." He repeated some of it in Icelandic. "Framan og bakinu."

The boat's engine was loud when Mikkel first cast off, though the noise of the water and the fog soon swallowed up sight or sound of it. I looked after it, watching for the exact moment when I could see it no longer, not even the hazy silhouette of it. The cove seemed too silent when it had left, even though the birds continued to call out and the tourists were talking and yelling occasionally.

"Briet." Runi's voice was soft but impatient. "Follow up after Pedró. Keep an eye out for the ferðamenn." He cocked a thumb towards the tourists, who were searching out their first steps on the steep Uppganga. They clung with tight hands to the ropes. "Maybe you tell the saga today," he said.

The words were casual. He was already turning back to the cliffs, moving to place a steadying hand on the waist of a middle-aged woman. But I could not stir at first, frozen still by Runi's suggestion. My face felt clammy and bloodless against the off-sea winds. When Grettir had defeated Glam—I could hear Jakop saying—he was afflicted with glámsýni, a fear of the night, which equated to a fear of things he could not see, things he only imagined. The fear I felt, sudden and violent, seemed to be irrational in this way, though I could not formulate or clearly determine what it was that I dreaded. My father's pronunciation of the word—glámsýni, glámsýni—sounded again and again in my head.

Now that I felt the fear and discomfort, it occurred to me that Drangey had harboured this angry, brooding air since we all had first stepped off the boat. Perhaps the fear was not something I had dug up out of myself but something I had come to recognize, like eyes adjusting to the dark. The cliffs, their dark faces scarred and mottled with white bird shit, waited, dull and heavy. I almost called out for Runi but could not think what I would tell him. Óheppni, bad luck. It would mean nothing to him. The tourists would ask for a translation, and what would they know of it? Perhaps the Icelanders among them would think fleetingly of Grettir.

I moved to the Uppganga and threw a bundle of net over my shoulder. It dug deep into my skin, even through the layers of my jacket and sweater. I threw out a hand, grabbing onto the rope rails, seeking the first step up. As my foot fell onto the grass-covered stone, it slipped, and I felt myself wavering. For a moment, the island darkened around me. The sky lowered, and green lights flickered and streaked across where before there had been clouds. The tourists, the ferðamenn, were gone. The other hunters were gone. The birds were gone. My heart pounded in my throat, and I held my breath without thinking of it. An eerie silence dripped from the rocks, trickling down my spine. I shouted, trying to shatter the quiet, but it would not be broken. My cry fell small and mute on the heavy air. The net slithered off my shoulder, and I let it go.

I might as well have been naked. The cold cut right through me. I moved out of desperation, throwing myself further up the Uppganga. There was blood on my hands. I could see it but not feel it. My grip was unsure on the rope and on the rocks.

"Pedró!" I yelled. "Runi!"

They did not answer. They were not there. Their absence was disturbing, but the lack of birds even more so. No ruffling feathers, no gurgling whistles in their fragile throats. I would think to catch a sight of uplifted wing, black and white, from the corner of my eye, and instead would catch dark sky, green lights, the looming threat of the she-troll on the water. The water was black.

A wind skimmed close to the ground on the top of Drangey. I could look out and see to the sky, unhindered by silhouette of man or animal. Tears stood in my eyes, and the wind stole them out.

"Briet, watch yourself." Runi's voice was sudden in my ear. I shook, and the world I knew came back to me. It had left me behind, and now it returned, bright fog and solid voice. My foot was on the edge of a dip in the ground, a hollow said to be a shelter for Grettir, living as an outlaw and banished on the lonely cliff.

"All right?" he asked.

I turned away, not answering. My hands were clean, wet but not bloodied. The net was gone from my shoulder. I clasped my hands together, trying to steady myself. Moving quickly, I went to the edge and looked down to the shore of the inlet, searching for the net. There was something there, on the black sand, but I could not make it out from this distance. It was white and daubed with brown, large and awkwardly sprawled.

"Runi," I said. "Runi, what did we leave behind?" The words, though I spoke them myself, echoed over in my head, disconnected.

He came over slowly, picking at his teeth with a toothpick, one eye on the tourists. The back of his neck was white and pale as he bent his head over to look. Looking at it, I thought of dead flesh, too well-preserved. He shook his head. "A bear?" he said.

We were twenty miles south of the Arctic Circle, and everyone knew that a polar bear had washed up on the shores just a little north of us not a year before. It was not something one expected, but having happened once, we had adopted it into our world view. Polar bears could come, and if they washed up delirious and hungry, they were dangerous and needed to be shot down.

"Is it moving?" Runi asked.

Pedró and Sveinn stayed with the tourists. They spoke loudly and laughed. The tourists' voices were constantly lilting upwards, questioning in more than one language. The birds were raucous. Runi climbed down first, and he was still grumbling at my insistence on coming. I followed, my feet close to his head as we descended.

"Don't go all the way down," I said. I stopped and looked down. Puffins nested in the rock near my ear. I could smell the wet feathers.

He glanced up at me and his mouth crooked at the corner, a look saying both *of course* and *you stay back if you're scared.*

"If it's alive, it could kill you."

"I know the day I'll die," he said, his voice now tense as he sought the next step. "And I'll be seventy-two and in bed with a woman not my wife."

"You know that?"

"I tell myself that. It'll be true enough."

"Just throw a stone," I said.

He scrabbled at the cliff and grabbed a handful of pebbles and crumbling rock. The puffins flung themselves lazily into the air. We heard a boat on the water. Runi looked up at me again, and now there was an air of concern.

"Throw them," I repeated. I clung closer to the rope, fearful that I would lose this Uppganga, the one noisy with birds and anxious Runi. Runi flung back his hand, holding awkwardly to the cliff, and slung the rocks at the mound of matted fur below. Now that we were closer, the object, the animal, seemed abnormally large, frighteningly huge relative to the puffins. It did not move as the small pebbles bounced off its body to the sand.

"It's dead," Runi said, but his voice was not as sure as when he'd predicted his own death.

We spoke as if we knew this was a polar bear, but there was doubt still. Runi climbed down. He stepped onto the sand. His pace was stilted and uneasy. I thumped to the ground behind him. Rocks crumbled under my boots. The sound grated in my ears, as if reality still rattled unsteady beneath me. Runi held his arm out to keep me from coming forwards. I knocked it out of the way, and he continued as if anxious to stay ahead of me.

With one foot, Runi kicked lightly at the broad, white-furred back. His boot left dark dirt enmeshed in the fur. The animal did not move. He kicked again, more violently this time. The whole bulk of the animal rocked forwards, then back.

"It's dead," he said.

I walked around to see the animal from the other side. From this angle, the fur and the bulk seemed a baggy coat over wasted flesh. The claws of the animal were broken and cracked short. The huge pads of its paws were white with salt-rime. Its head was buried into the rocks. I bent over and grabbed the flesh of its head and its ear and tugged it up. I dropped it immediately, shivering, wanting to throw up my breakfast. My stomach jolted like I was riding a boat into the trench of a large wave.

"Eh," Runi queried, and moved to join me. He imitated me, lifting up the head. He dropped it again and swallowed visibly.

The face was hard to reconcile with the rest of the bear. For it seemed a polar bear in every other way. But the hair of its face had fallen away in patches, leaving large areas of exposed flesh. The flesh was pocked with blood and sores, crusted with scabs half peeled away by the sea. In an odd way, furless as it was, it seemed more like a man's face, aged and wounded, poorly shaved, with a protruding jaw and nose. Some other mammal, a seal perhaps, had eaten away at the revealed flesh. This made the face of the bear smaller and, again, more human.

"Poor bastard," Runi said, as a way of breaking the shallow-breathed tension. But this did not help me. Because Runi would not say this of a puffin or of a bear. He would say it of a man.

The eyes of the bear were open and black. I thought I could see green lights reflected in them, and I looked to Runi and threw my head back to see the arm of a tourist flung out over the cliff edge with a smartphone. The rocks crumbled under our feet again as we turned, hearing the boat closer now, rounding the she-troll.

"She's something," Mikkel said, after he had herded the tourists towards the Uppganga, shouting at them to stop staring at the bloated body. He shouted in Icelandic so only half could understand. The other half might still tip him something when he brought them back to their campers and parked cars. "That will work for a drink or two." He did not know the bear was female.

"Face like a nightmare," Runi said. He laughed now, but it seemed at odds with our initial revulsion. I could not laugh or smile.

The sky darkened again, and a blast of wind from off the sea smacked my face. I stumbled backwards and found myself falling. The rocks were hard beneath me. I was alone. The green lights were there in the sky, as if the reflection in the bear's eyes had predicted them. I raised a hand to my mouth and bit my knuckle to keep from screaming. The waves were crashing hard into the cove, and the water was littered with something white and black and small. They were feathers, choking the water, thick and slick, washing up with every sweep of black water. I tasted bile in my throat.

I glanced around desperately, hoping to see a tourist or Runi or Mikkel. Where the bear had been, there was a shadowy mass of fur, wrinkled and matted. It was cloaking something, covering it away from the wind and the lights. My heart beat fast, fluttering at my throat. I crawled to my feet but still stayed close to the ground, stretching my hands out to balance my crouching stance. With quick, furtive turns of my head, I checked left, right, and behind. The feeling of something watching me was heavy and humid in the air. Out at sea, the she-troll lumbered up through the waves, and there was something of metamorphosis about her rocky haunches, as if she were melting slowly to flesh, reversing the effects of the sun that had frozen her to stone. Her husband was still lost to the time and water that had swallowed him.

I crept towards the fur. With one finger, I touched it, and it was soft and smooth. The salt of the sea and the matted blood had disappeared. Then, my whole hand. I laid it flat and could feel the hard outlines of a body beneath the fur. I looked again up, behind, right and left. The she-troll's stone grew rosy and fleshy under the green light. I yanked away the fur as if I might pull back the curtain between my world and this, as if it might hasten my return.

A man lay curled on the sand. He was naked and thin so that his ribs stuck out beneath his pointed elbow. I thought he must be dead. He was unmoving. So I did not move my hand back. I left it hovering in the air above his head. But then he stirred. I sprang to my feet. The man craned his head without moving his body, searching with his eyes. Finally, he bent his neck back and I could see the wrinkled skin at the nape. He looked at me. I felt cold. Glam, the undead returned unholy. This was all I could think. His skin glistened as if freshly healed from extensive wounds. His eyes were large and black with very little white. I could not move as he watched me. Eventually his mouth opened. His tongue lolled out, wet, so that saliva glittered in the corners of his lips.

It felt like my chest tore open. Muscles peeled back, ribs and lungs left exposed and aching. And I cried, though I would not say to myself why. The man reached out a hand, and the fur fell back from his shoulders. His nails were long but cracked. They were familiar to me.

I heard steps behind me.

"Light-headed, are you?" Runi shoved my shoulder.

"Leave me be," I said. I was almost unhappy to see him.

The roads were lonely between the farm and Sauðárkrókur. The headlights flickered on and past the stones and grass grown close up on the road. I gripped the wheel tightly. The music on the radio, though turned up to an ear-shaking volume, sounded soft and distant to me.

I pulled the car in near to the house, opened and slammed shut the driver's door. I rattled the keys in my hand and found the one to the back door by feel. Stars shone low on the horizon. The blinds on the door window slammed against the glass when I closed it. Now, out of the car, every noise seemed unnaturally loud.

My jacket I draped over a chair at the kitchen table. There was an empty soup can near the stove, unrinsed like the pan.

"Pabbi," I yelled out, not so much because I thought he would shout back but because it was my way of telling him I was home.

The stairs creaked under me when I went upstairs. Here, the hall was short, but the lights were out, and it felt longer in the dark. My father's door was cracked open, and there was a sliver of light all round the frame. I stared at it.

"Pabbi," I said again, and listened to the silence which answered.

I imagined him telling the story in the light of that room ahead, pretending we sat in the sunlight and the grass and the wind on top of Drangey. Grettir grinned out at me from the dim corners. He was waiting and laughing at the idea of fated death. He whetted the blade of his axe, and the noise was a whistle, high and keen.

I turned back and went down the stairs to the kitchen. I rinsed out the can and threw it into the garbage. I put the pan to soak in the sink. Then I slipped into the chair. It was glámsýni, and I could see nothing good in the hallway, could not force myself to go further.

Because it would be worse, I thought, to go in and not have him reach his hand out towards me.

CALIFORNIAN ILLUSION

Abner Porzio

Abner Porzio *very recently had his poem 'The Boiling River', selected for publication in the poetry anthology* Aurora—The Allegory Ridge Poetry Anthology *(Volume 02). His sestina 'Watch Winter Fall Up' was published in* The Road Not Taken: The Journal of Formal Poetry *(Fall 2019, Volume 13, Issue 3). Abner's first publication, his sonnet 'The Fastest Five Finger Roulette Ever', was in the international magazine* New Poetry. *He graduated in 2013 from Arizona State University's undergraduate creative writing program (poetry), where he was a poetry editor for* Superstition Review *(Issue 12).*

Californian Illusion

Heiress to the Winchester rifle manufacturer,
Sarah L Winchester, the only resident of a 160 acre Californian estate,
provided 24 hour days of work; 20 carpenters, 20 servants
       built 160 rooms, 1200 window frames,
1000 cabinets, 40 staircases, 950 doors, 52 skylights and
       40 bedrooms for 38 consecutive years.

Hijinx or bust;
       excessive homebody building.

She'd run up the jumble of Victorian castle's
       spiral stairs that led nowhere.
At midnight, a bell rang from her séance tower.
Web patterned, beveled stained glass crystal windows
       bore Shakespearean words:
       Wide Unclasp~The Tables Of~
       Their Thoughts~These Same~Thoughts People~
       This Little World

Sarah prayed for redemption for her deceased children.

The widow had crossed her heart and hoped to die for
      atonement with the masses of Indians
         killed with the gun that won the West.
Buffalo Bill's most prized model: the Winchester '73.
According to Mrs Winchester,
her Venus flytrap of a thirteen-story observatory tower
      snacked on trespassing demons.

Clear blueprints, ongoing contracts
had been written to herself on napkins. Rumours have it
      that she was possessed by ghosts —little Indian ghouls.
And that Sarah had struck a deal with the dead: the extension
of her lifetime for the compliance to a never-ending construction.
At 85 years of age,
the recluse died face down
      on her organ in her empty grand ballroom.

DARK AND STORMY

Mike Gillis

Mike Gillis *is the head writer of* The Onion. *His writing has been published in* The New Yorker, McSweeney's, ClickHole, *and the* Chicago Quarterly Review. *He was born in Maine, went to school in New Hampshire, and, as of this writing, is alive in Chicago.*

$\mathcal{D}$ARK AND STORMY

It was a dark and stormy night.

Well, not exactly stormy. More mildly drizzling. And given that there was a full moon, it's fair to say that it wasn't quite dark out, either. It's more accurate to say that it was poorly lit. Fine. But "it was a poorly lit and mildly drizzling night" doesn't exactly roll off the tongue, now does it? Doesn't quite conjure the wonderful picture of a dark and stormy night. Also, pardon me for trying to give you a little *dramatic suspense*, your royal highness. Why does everything have to be a perfectly accurate picture of reality? Aren't you reading this to escape from your woebegotten life for a few measly hours?

For Christ's sake.

Well, anyway, it was a poorly lit and mildly drizzling night (*happy* now?) and our protagonist was taking shelter in a ditch off the side of the road. Okay, it wasn't quite a ditch, either. I guess a culvert? Is a culvert more exact here? I'm actually not sure. Or is it a storm drain? Hold on a second — let me just flip the dictionary open and check it out. This'll only take a second.

Culver's Root … culverin …

Okay, great. Here it is. "*Cul-vert:* a drain or covered channel that crosses under a road, railway, et cetera ..." So, no, that's actually not the right word, come to think of it. He's more in a tent. Yeah, a tent. That's the ticket. Honestly, I don't know why I was thinking culvert or ditch. Those are way off. But what are you going to do, get angry at me? Like this is so easy? Well, if so, you can screw right off.

Jesus Christ, you think you can narrate better than this? Do you? It's a goddamn *tough* position to be in, just narrating things off the top of your head. Meanwhile, you're probably patting yourself on the back just for reading this so well. Well, congratulations on being literate, you prick.

Alright, alright. I'm sorry for getting angry at you.

Look, it's been a hard couple of months at work. When I first got this job as a narrator, it was sincerely like a dream come true. But, lately, my boss has really been riding my ass. All his feedback is negative. Too "omniscient" here, too "limited" there. It's like I cannot please this guy. Does he seriously think this is easy? That I roll out of bed and immediately peer into someone's mind and render a series of events into a coherent storyline, just like that?

Anyway, after getting chewed out a few dozen times, I started taking a nip or two of Scotch in the morning before I got into the Narration Office. Just to take the edge off, you know? And so now I start thinking things are going really great, since I'm bombed half the time. But suddenly, one day, I can't remember if so-and-so's story is first-person or third-person or, hell, if I'm actually supposed to be in second person the whole time. And then I kind of puked all over my notes, and he saw. I guess he saw because I also puked on his lap and kind of cursed him out and badmouthed his son and so forth. So, hey, I'll admit that was my bad. But did I deserve to be demoted all the way down to narrating supermarket-aisle-quality fantasy storylines like this one?

No. No goddamn way.

Look, would the greats of narration be ashamed of me if they saw what kind of low-grade narrative work I was doing here? Sure. I don't think the guys and gals who narrated *Don Quixote* or *Anna Karenina* or *Orlando* would see me pat-drying vomit off my narration notes in the office men's room and say "that man is destined for great things."

My wife left me, too. Jesus. Mary just up and left. She's staying at her sister's until this blows over, but I think she's going to come back and pack her stuff, take the kids—just leave. God, I wanted my son to be a narrator just like me. Now what's he going to be? Some sort of lowly Greek chorus member? Screw that. I'd rather die. I'm serious.

The sad irony of this all is that Mary was the one who wanted me to become a narrator in the first place. She said she'd always seen in me an incredible knack for narration, a kind of innate talent for knitting together the disparate events of the world into a seamless whole. There were these gorgeous summer nights years ago when we first met in college—you don't need to hear about this, but whatever—when she would trace little figure-eights over my chest and tell me the sort of narrator I'd become. We'd be lying in the grass, the two of us, with these soft orange daubs of distant classrooms blooming through the twilight, bullbats flapping off into the purple sky, and she would whisper into my ear how omniscient my narration could be if I just worked at it. If I just really cared about something for once. If I close my eyes, I can still feel those warm New England zephyrs blowing over me, the moths gliding across the wet grass, and the cool impression of her breath as she said that my stream of consciousness contained multitudes. Yet here I am, wondering if I even care anymore.

Where was I? Oh, right.

It was a dark and stormy night. Our protagonist was sitting in a tent, and somewhere, very far away, a disgraced narrator was opening up a fresh bottle of Glen Logie Blended Scotch and hoping beyond hope that this little story would distract him from the horrible, aching absence in his life.

Mary, I love you. Please come back.

GHOST STORY

SL Leong

Sylvia Leong is a therapeutic personal trainer and passionate environmentalist living in a cottage in the sky, amid the rainforest of North Vancouver. The city itself and the surrounding ravines and mountains serve as inspiration for her uplifting stories about myth and magic. 'Ghost Story' is her first published fiction. It first appeared in Imagination: cc&d magazine (volume 297, May 2020). Otherwise, her fiction, non-fiction, and blog are listed at slleong.com.

Ghost Story

I was ten years old when a ghost tore a rent in my spine and sifted into my body. Not a physical rent — not through the skin, not through the bones, but through a different dimension.

I only knew of abstract ideas like dimensions because my brother Jasper was obsessed with science fiction-y things. A drawing on a piece of paper was two-dimensional. Humans lived in the third dimension. Time was the fourth dimension. This ghost was something else altogether.

"Chloe." A warm hand shook my shoulder. "Chloe, wake up."

I peeled my face from my pink, crocheted bedspread. My book, a story about a leprechaun and a unicorn, lay open next to me. I'd fallen asleep. But it hadn't been a dream; I could feel the ghost. It was like a presence keeping me company — from the inside.

"Don't be afraid," Jasper whispered.

I gazed into Jasper's midnight-blue eyes, his face framed with dark curls, his colouring the exact match of mine. Should I tell him? But then the ghost caressed me, letting me know her presence wasn't evil. It felt good and kind, like Julie Andrews in Mom's favourite movie, *The Sound of Music*.

"Come with me," Jasper said. "There's something I want to show you."

We crept down the hall through a fog of tension. They always fought quietly. Dad's hushed accusations hurled through clenched teeth. Mom's silence; she was an expert at taking a beating.

It always tied me up inside.

The fighting and the beatings didn't happen often, but the tension grew daily, like a red balloon inflating until, without warning, it burst, leaving curled red pieces lying everywhere.

The back porch's floorboards creaked under our weight. A ramshackle garage took up half the backyard, leaning to one side as though propped on an elbow. The grey wood with its peeling white paint gleamed in the rising moonlight.

Except for a broom, the garage was empty. Jasper swept the concrete until drifts of dirt clung to the walls and climbed the corners. He put his hands to the floor, pushed off with his feet, and distracted me with handstands performed to perfection.

"Come on, Chloe. You try."

The concrete was cold beneath my splayed fingers. I kicked up hard, and Jasper caught my ankles. Blood rushed to my head. I was doing a handstand!

A few months after our garage gymnastics, Mom was in a car crash and admitted to Lions Gate Hospital. Each day beneath falling autumn leaves, I walked up to visit her.

I held her hand, wanting to tell her about the ghost, wishing I'd told her before, but she was unconscious. In critical condition, they said. Mom's dark hair, longer than Jasper's, curled around her milk-white face — a face that each day I burned deeper into memory. The hollow inside me grew; the ghost swirled within.

A nurse wearing lavender scrubs walked in and checked a beeping machine on one side of the bed. A brassy strand sprang from her messy bun, waving as she tucked the covers securely under Mom's chin. With a cotton ball, she wiped the shine from Mom's face. My heart glowed at her ministrations.

"Ooh," the nurse said. "The back of your arm's twitching."

I held it out. "It's been doing that for months. Sometimes long twitches, sometimes short."

Her pinkie finger brushed over the puckering dimple. "Your tricep muscle's fasciculating." She drew a notebook from the pocket of her shirt and scratched pen over paper. "You need more potassium, calcium, and magnesium in your diet." She tore off the page. "Here."

> *Bananas*
> *White beans*
> *Spinach*
> *Cheese*
> *Whole wheat bread*

In that instant, I decided to be a nurse. I wanted to tell people the proper food to eat. I wanted to help people who'd been in car crashes. I wanted to wear something as comfortable as pyjamas to work.

Mom never came home. A few months later, Dad started giving Mom's beatings to Jasper, leaving bruises where no one could see. Jasper was twelve.

Afterwards, Dad would leave Jasper clutching his middle and lying on the hardwood floor. I'd hover around my brother until he barked at me to get lost. Even so, he never got physical. In the hospital, when Mom had finally woken, she'd made him promise never to hit a woman. She made him promise just before she died.

Morse Code

"Morse code is a slow way to communicate," said Bobby Gregor during his sixth-grade presentation. "For example, if a truck was hurtling towards your friend, you wouldn't use Morse code to warn him."

Everyone in the class giggled.

As Bobby continued, I was distracted by the back of my arm fasciculating like crazy. I slapped my hand overtop to hide the spasms from my classmates. No matter what I ate or how much water I drank, it always came back. A panicked vibration, especially when I did something naughty like pilfer an apple in the lunch line at school.

"Each letter of the alphabet is communicated through its own combination of dots and dashes." Bobby clicked the large screen to an international Morse code chart. "And there's a long pause between each word."

Dots and dashes, long twitches and short twitches, both with long pauses in between. The language of my ghost.

In the school library, I found a book on Morse code and flipped the pages until I found a chart. With my pencil poised over my notebook, I whispered, "Who are you?"

Twitches, long and short, dimpled my tricep. I filled the note-book with dots and dashes. "Slow down," I pleaded in a whisper.

Finally, the twitching stopped, and I set to translating. M-I-N-A-D-A-W-S-O-N. Mina Dawson. Weird. All this time I'd been calling her Julie. "Did you live in North Vancouver?" The fasciculation started again. My home address.

"What do you want?"

"Only to help."

MUSEUM AND ARCHIVES

The bus stop on Grand Boulevard was as crowded as I'd hoped. I chose a lady with dark hair and stayed close, boarding the 228 *Lynn Valley* as though I were her daughter, as though the bus were my personal chariot. With so many passengers getting on, the driver didn't notice I hadn't paid. But Mina noticed, and my tricep vibrated with anger.

I got off at the North Vancouver Museum and Archives.

When I walked in, the librarian—head tilted, mouth open—stared. My small stature made me look eight, maybe nine on a brave day. She held a rotary phone in one hand, the receiver halfway to her ear. She set it back on the phone's cradle.

"Hi, I'm Shirles. How can I help?" A royal blue scarf wrapped her neck and trailed over her black shirt. One stray tawny hair clung to her shoulder.

"I'm looking for information on Mina Dawson of North Vancouver. It's for a grade six report." I lied easily and often, but only when necessary.

Shirles sat me down at a long table with many chairs, and brought me a cup of water. I sipped the cool water until she returned with an armful of paper. In a museum newsletter, text wrapped two yellowed photos, both of old houses owned by Mina and her two sisters and used as hospitals between 1910 and 1918.

The next document was the *North Vancouver Express*, dated September 11, 1908. Shirles tapped her finger on an ad: *Misses Dawson for the North Vancouver Hospital: $17.50 to $20 per week and city patients, $1 per day.* Man, oh man, things were cheap back then.

Another page from the same newspaper listed exhibition awards: Mina Dawson won first prize for doilies, knit lace, and drawn work, and second prize for crochet.

"So old-fashioned," I whispered, giggling. Mina gave a long twitch that was more like a pinch.

Then last, but not least, Shirles delicately finessed an old photo in front of me. And there was Mina Dawson: short curls, a long nose, and no make-up whatsoever. She was wearing an ankle-length dress with a white hat and apron — an old-fashioned nurses' uniform. Mina gave a shiver of recognition; a thrill coursed through me. Mina had been a nurse. I was definitely going to be a nurse.

"It wasn't customary to smile for pictures back then," Shirles said.

"Oh." I nodded.

Shirles photocopied everything and sent me on my way with a pat on the back and best wishes for my school report.

Fancy

We lived on East 1st Street in one of the middling blocks between Lonsdale and Moodyville Park. The old house was close enough to the grain export terminal to hear the whirring and banging, close enough to the railroad to hear the screeching of metal wheels against metal tracks and to be woken by the terrific slam as railcars were shunted.

The day after my sixteenth birthday, a windstorm overturned a tree. It rested across our jaundiced lawn, taking up the other half of the backyard, roots exposed and wagging in the now-gentle breeze. There'd been no point in removing it because our house was the only one left standing amongst the rubble. A property development company had cleared blocks and blocks of houses to make way for fancy new townhomes and condominiums.

Fancy was Dad's word. "This used to be a decent area for hard-working folk before it started getting all fancy," he grouched.

Dad was a millwright journeyman down at the grain export terminal. We didn't expect him home for another hour. Following every shift, he'd hit the pub. Like a monogamous barfly, he'd patronize *one* drinking establishment—until he did or said something that got him banned. Then he'd move on to another.

On the concrete floor of the ramshackle garage, Jasper finished a set of push-ups. "I've been granted a partial scholarship to SFU," he said, squatting back on his heels. "The downtown campus. I can take the SeaBus across the harbour." Jasper had decided to be an editor.

"Congratulations!"

Mina twisted with joy inside me.

He put his finger to his lips. "It's a secret, right?"

I nodded. We had a month of school before summer break.

He leapt, grasped the rafters, and pumped out one chin-up after another. Dad walked around the corner, into the garage's open doorway. Jasper dropped to his feet and squared his shoulders. I edged towards the door, my insides knotting.

"This is what you've been up to!" Dad ducked back into the alleyway, and returned with a greying two-by-four. "Puffing yourself up, all fancy-like. You think you're so strong," he sneered. "I'll show you who's a man and who's a pussy."

A rusty nail glinted in the sunshine. Dad whipped his arms above his head then thrust the wood down on Jasper.

I screamed.

Jasper caught the wood, ripped it out of Dad's hands, and hurled it into the alley. Dad shrank before my eyes, and Jasper grew bigger.

Before Jasper could turn around, Dad's fists were already flying. It was the first time he'd beaten Jasper outside the house. It was the first time he'd left a mark where someone could see.

Jasper knelt on hands and knees, blood and spit dripping from his mouth.

A pale copper key chimed against the concrete. A dirty envelope skidded to a halt beside it. "Our fancy new home." Dad stalked away, shouting. "It's more than I can afford."

I lurched towards Jasper. "You've been *letting* him beat you up!"

He staggered to his feet, his face a mess — eye swollen and bottom lip puffy, his chin covered in blood as thick and red as raspberry jam. He stepped towards me, looming. "If he can't beat me," Jasper hissed, "who do you think he's going after next?" The truth slugged me in the stomach.

His fear for me shone in his eyes. Even so, he flicked a hand and stomped off.

I wrenched open the garage door to go after him. But then my tricep twitched, the long and short bursts of a warning. After six years with Mina, I understood her immediately.

"Give Jasper a moment to collect himself. He's hurting, physically and mentally. Lashing out was only a reaction, a misguided attempt to lessen his own pain."

I closed the door and leaned against it.

Mina was never shy about sharing her wisdom. Over the years, she'd said over and over, *"Choose from a place of love, not fear."* When I was younger, I'd no idea what she meant. Once I understood, I rebelled anyway, doing the opposite of whatever she wanted and suffering the consequences. It wasn't long before Mina's guidance became more concise: *"You don't have to treat people the way your father treats you. A fight takes two people. Let the anger end here."* I'd learned to follow her advice, and my relationship with Jasper benefited, which made life much easier. Life was difficult enough.

After a while, my breathing lost its little gasps and became steady. My heart slowed. The sick feeling dissipated and was replaced with something more centred.

I retrieved the key from the concrete floor and slid it onto my key chain. Two pieces of paper inhabited the dirty envelope: our eviction notice and a rental agreement.

"Now that you're in a better frame of mind," Mina said, *"go find him. Tend the wounds on his face."*

At Mina's behest, I kept a first aid kit in a square basket stocked with stolen supplies. I found Jasper at the kitchen table, staring at his feet. Dad wasn't around.

I dabbed hydrogen peroxide on the cuts on Jasper's face as he read the papers. "Let's take a look at our *fancy* new home," he said.

A ten-minute walk brought us to a three-story walk-up painted lemon yellow. The key opened the front door of its studio apartment. The malt-coloured carpet had cigarette burns and was sticky with spills. Food smeared the chocolate-brown cupboard doors. Someone had tried to dump vegetable soup down the kitchen sink.

"Who would have thought," said Jasper, shaking his head, "that the most expensive part of living would be a place to sleep. The opposite of Dickensian times, you know." He glanced at me. "Back then, food was expensive and rent was cheap."

I spun slowly, tears welling. Dad expected me to clean this up.

Mina ghosted up my spine, trying to soothe me.

"I won't be living here." Jasper placed a hand on my shoulder. "And Chloe, you won't either." He shrugged out of his kangaroo jacket, wrapped it around his fist, and quietly slammed a hole into the gyproc. "A little present for Dad," Jasper said, massaging his hand. "Come with me. There's something I want to show you."

THE RAVINE

Our high school, Greyson Secondary, was perched near the edge of a ravine. Even so, over the school year, surprisingly few students ambled the paths into the lush foliage, probably too immersed in technology to consider it. I followed Jasper down the winding trail, under sunlit leaves.

As kids, we used to play in a broken-down hut hidden in the thick foliage on the ravine's northernmost incline. I hadn't seen it in years. Jasper and I ducked around the last post of the wooden bridge and climbed down to the stream. We trudged the pebbly shoreline near the slope and walked deeper into the forest.

Our hut had been transformed. It stood upright and sturdy, and the wall boards and shingles were mostly new.

"Trent and I repaired this," Jasper said. Trent was Jasper's best buddy. His father owned a contracting company that had made 'thick bucks off the fancy folks' thanks to gentrification.

"I'm living here while I go to school," Jasper said. "You can too … if you want?"

I blinked. My mouth dropped open. Could we sink any lower?

"*Steady, Chloe,*" Mina said. "*Keep your thoughts to yourself. Focus on how hard he's worked.*"

"Uh … Jas." I splayed my open palm against one of the boards. "It's so sturdy. You've done a great job."

Jasper, grinning with pride, fumbled with the padlock securing the door. The inside of the hut was bare and smelled of freshly cut wood. Jasper unlatched and swung open four sets of shutters. The sun slanted in from the west, brightening the small space. "We positioned the windows so we could look out in every direction."

"Smart." I scanned the walls—no electrical outlets. My stomach bottomed out.

"It's just a place to sleep, Chloe," Jasper said as though reading my thoughts. "We can study at school or the library." He shrugged. "Or coffee shops with free wi-fi. We'll brush our teeth, shower, and fill our water bottles at the community centre. I'll get us memberships."

I gazed out the back window at a massive hemlock and imagined nights in the hut. Weighed it against the studio apartment. Against being beaten.

"You'll adjust, I promise," Mina said, but she swirled and twisted inside me.

"You'll finally have a gym," I said, turning. "Plus, I won't have to cook."

"We won't have dad's food allowance anymore." Jasper cleared his throat. "But we can probably keep buying things like apples and oranges. Bananas too. And we'll use my server discount at Surf's Up! and eat at our schools' cafeterias."

Mina spun around my heart and lifted my spirits. *"We can make this work,"* she said. Determination surged through me.

That night, back at the house, Dad hadn't come home yet. When he was really angry, he'd overstay his welcome at the pub and come home even later than usual, ready to fight again.

My bedroom door had a lock; Jasper's didn't. So together we dragged his mattress, blankets, and pillows onto the floor of my bedroom. I set his water glass and cell phone on my makeshift night table, a metallic pink skate case.

"You'll make someone a great wife one day," Jasper said, watching me, smiling.

I wrinkled my nose. "Or nurse."

"Probably both."

I fell asleep to the lull of Jasper's gentle snores.

We woke to Dad crashing and banging down the hall. Jasper's bedroom door squeaked open. Then Dad rattled my doorknob, and when it wouldn't give, he pounded on the wood, his hits dulled by alcohol.

The next morning, Dad whistled. He stirred sugar into his coffee, acting as though nothing had happened, and yet he did not look Jasper in the face. Although it wouldn't change anything if he remembered, I hoped he was ashamed.

Shopping

On the third day of summer vacation, Dad left for work early. We packed everything we needed. It didn't take long.

Trent pulled up to the house in one of his father's trucks. My heart pirouetted as it always did when I saw him. He had the sort of look girls swooned over: ice-blue eyes, shoulder-length, soft blond waves, and a powerful body that countered the prettiness of his face.

The truck's bed held our mattresses, an old steamer trunk, a pine wine rack, and my skate case. Shoes, clothes, hangers, towels, and bathroom totes were thrown in loose. Jasper and Trent hid the truck in Trent's father's garage and spent the afternoon playing video games.

I went on a shopping spree.

A box with an image of a black metal bowl, its sides shaped into branches, caught my eye. Rustic and beautiful, it made me think of our forest. We deserved nice things just like everyone else. I slid the box from the shelf and placed it in the cart beside Mom's old tangerine purse.

Hidden in an aisle piled high with wicker baskets, I opened the box and cursed under my breath; crinkly plastic wrapped the bowl. I returned the box to the buggy and flung a cushion overtop to hide the open packaging. My tricep muscle vibrated, and continued to twitch in little pinches as I strolled to the electronics area and watched *Die Hard*.

"Stop it, Mina," I whispered. "I'm doing this. You'll only distract me and get us caught." She went quiet. When the explosions in the movie started, I reached inside the box, and in one smooth motion, yanked off the plastic wrap and stuffed it beneath the bowl.

In the dishware aisle, I held a tumbler up to the light and squinted through the glass, disguising my search for the security camera. I turned my back to it and tested the heft of a water jug before placing it in the cart. I reached inside the box and smoothly tucked the bowl into the tangerine purse, then flung the cushion, covering the open packaging.

My pulse raced.

I stopped in the middle of another isle and closed the empty box while running one hand through wind chimes. Then I approached a clerk stocking towels and asked, "Would it be okay if I used the washroom?"

"Down the hall and to the left."

"Would you mind watching my cart?"

Her eyebrow arched. Then she broke our gaze, murmured an unreliable, "Sure," and with a jerk, placed the last towel on the shelf.

I grabbed my purse from the cart and held it in front of my body as I sauntered down the hall. It's always the things happening right in front of us we never see.

In the bathroom stall, I rearranged my purse so the pointed edges of the bowl faced inward, the bottom smooth with the leather.

"Proud of yourself?" asked Mina.

"Yes, it was a perfect performance. And I feel much better now." Grinning, I bowed before the full-length mirror next to the bathroom door.

Mina swirled.

I bolted via the emergency exit into the sunshine, the alarm thundering in my ears like applause.

JASPER AND TRENT

Late that evening, I stood on the wooden bridge over the ravine, shining the flashlight through the blackness onto the pebbles of the shore.

Jasper and Trent manoeuvred one of our twin-sized mattresses down the incline and over several fallen trees. We'd been using the same ones since before Mom had died. Jasper's feet had been hanging off the end for years.

I tromped ahead, the oval of my flashlight leading our way. While holding it in my teeth, I shoved a key into the padlock.

"Don't hit your head on the dowel, Chloe," Jasper said. Inside, a wooden pole had been affixed above the door, extending to the window across.

"What's it for?"

"Hanging clothes." That explained the many hangers he'd collected from the house. I stepped back as they stooped to get the mattress through the narrow door. "To the right side, Trent, on top of the tarp," Jasper grunted. With a muffled thump and swoosh of air, the mattress found its home.

Jasper lit a kerosene lantern.

Trent's beautiful face twisted in a grimace and he growled, "Why are there two tarps?" He glared at me.

I recoiled, perplexed.

"I can't leave her with him," Jasper whispered. "You know what he'll do." His voice wavered, just like it did when I was eleven and he told me about the birds and the bees.

"But you said we'd …" Trent stomped his foot then pushed past Jasper. But Jasper's hand darted out and grabbed Trent's … and held it.

"Oh!" I said, as the nature of their relationship became clear. "Oh!" Dad would kill Jasper. Trent's dad would kill them both.

Jasper rested his forehead on his open palm; red patches crawled up his neck. I swallowed hard.

"*Give them a few minutes alone,*" commanded Mina, swirling.

"I'll, uh …" I whispered. "I'll go wait in the truck."

The curtain of clothes, hung for privacy, didn't quite reach the ends of our mattresses. The open space became our makeshift parlour, and after Trent said his goodbyes, that is where Jasper and I sat, facing one another. A pine wine-rack, stuffed with our shoes, stood to one side of the door. The oversized, tangerine purse held our bathroom totes and hung from a nail above. An old steamer trunk had our sweaters, winter gear, books, and laptops inside; the lantern and bowl sat atop. My skate case held our underwear.

Our fancy new home.

"What's with the fancy new bowl, klepto?" Jasper asked, gesturing to the branch bowl atop the steamer trunk.

"Where else will we put our fruit?" I shrugged.

"The surest way to fuck up our careful existence is by you getting caught shoplifting."

The danger to our *careful existence* should have been Dad, but he wouldn't even look for us. Jasper was of age, and Dad knew I'd stay with him.

I shrugged and promised to rein in my talents. Unless, of course, they became necessary.

WINTER

Massive dryers rattled behind me. As I folded our clean clothes on the laminate countertop, Jasper stuffed them into the pink skate case and tangerine purse.

We walked up Lonsdale Avenue through freshly fallen snow and towards the ravine. The tangerine bag hung heavily across my body, and the skate case rested on Jasper's shoulder. I wasn't looking forward to sleep. As the weather had grown colder, we'd added more blankets. Tonight, I wasn't sure if they would be enough.

We entered the ravine, now an enchanted, snow-covered forest, the iron-grey afternoon light rendering it dim and mysterious. We heard the city park stewards before we saw them. Jasper stopped short.

"It's like someone lives here," a male voice said. Then a clunk, as though he'd lifted the padlock and let it fall.

"The windows have shutters," a female voice called out, mingling with the sounds of rustling brush and snapping branches. "But they're latched on the inside."

I shifted on my feet, wanting to scream at them, wanting to beat them up, wanting to make them leave.

"*Steady, Chloe,*" Mina said. "*Just wait and watch.*"

"Let's get the bolt cutters," the male voice said.

"Let's not," she said. "It's happy hour, eh? We can pretend we didn't find this until Monday."

Jasper tugged my coat sleeve and backed us silently behind a cypress. We sat on the skate case, the tangerine bag behind us, and watched as the stewards reached the bridge and disappeared into the denim-blue dusk.

That evening, Jasper lay on his mattress, brooding into a novel.

"*Let him alone,*" Mina ghosted along my spine.

We slept in our coats and under all our blankets.

On Saturday, when I woke, Jasper was gone.

I remembered the park stewards, and my insides plunged. We couldn't stay here. And I couldn't imagine what we'd do.

I knew that back at the store, on the shelf above the branch bowls, sat three black votives. They would look so homey with tea lights flickering inside. I yearned for them, but I'd made my promise to Jasper.

The city library was warm. I was finishing a project due on Monday when Jasper found me in my favourite carrel.

"Come with me," he said. "There's something I want to show you."

Out on Lonsdale Avenue, a camper nestled in the bed of an old pickup truck. Jasper opened the back door and stepped inside, gesturing for me to follow.

"It'll be warmer, anyway," he said.

I blinked. "Whose?" We didn't have money earmarked for this.

"Mine. All mine."

"You used up your savings for next semester?"

"I can take a semester off."

In that instant, the burden balanced on Jasper's shoulders became visible: the weight of his education, the weight of his job, the weight of his relationship with Trent. The weight of taking care of me.

"Thank you." I opened my hands, knowing I should say more, wishing I were eloquent enough to do so. Then I realized I'd thanked Jasper on my own, without Mina's prodding.

"It'll be more expensive living this way — insurance and gas. But I got you a job at Surf's Up! The Saturday morning shift … if you want."

"Of course." The idea of working, of contributing, felt good, felt right.

"Trent will help us move our stuff when it gets dark."

Muscles that I hadn't even realized were tense now relaxed. "No one can evict us." Gratitude spiked and settled into my heart. The branch bowl would look perfect on the countertop by the sink. I could cook again.

Jasper smirked in agreement. "No, Chloe, we'll never be evicted again, but we'll have to keep moving. Park in different locations."

"Behind the mall with the rest of the motor homes."

"Who would've thought we'd end up there?" Jasper laughed and clapped a hand on my shoulder. "Well, klepto, you've got a year and a half left of high school, then on to nursing college. Living in this," he said, waving around the interior of the camper, "I think we're going to make it."

When I'd had a home, an actual house, I couldn't imagine how it felt to *not* have one: how unsettling, how unsafe. Now, with this new home awaiting us, a warm blanket of safety draped over me and filled the hollow inside — the hollow where Mina lived. She swirled around, caressing me in a ghostly goodbye. I would miss her, but I was ready; I no longer needed her. Mina left through my spine and returned back home, into her own dimension.

THE HUMMINGBIRD FLASH FICTION PRIZE

THE 2021 HUMMINGBIRD FLASH FICTION PRIZE

Every year, the Hummingbird contest opens in spring and culminates in summer, with the stories offered to you in winter. And, as I write these words on a blustery day in autumn, an intrepid Anna's hummingbird is sipping at the backyard vermillionaire. He will likely spend winter here in the North's cold climes.

We are delighted to share with you the winners of this year's Hummingbird Flash Fiction Prize. Like the contest for which they are named, these stories are tenacious but tender—and, like my backyard visitor, will linger all year long.

First Place:
'The Weeping Pools' by **Cadence Mandybura**

First Runner-Up:
'River's Thousand-One Voice' by **Cadence Mandybura**

Second Runner-Up:
'Glimpse of a Goddess' by **Laura Kuhlmann**

Judge Bob Thurber had this to say about the winners: *The clarity, strength, and serenity of 'The Weeping Pools', with its restrained composition, nudged it just ahead of 'River's Thousand-One Voice', which I enjoyed very much for its lovely voice. Also, and not least, the very concise 'Glimpse of a Goddess' has considerable merit. Congratulations to all the finalists.*

Thank you to Bob for once again lending us his keen and discerning eye. Congratulations to the winning authors and the other shortlisted entrants in the 2021 Hummingbird Flash Fiction Prize:

Andrew Moore for 'Ye Fair in the Wood'
Andrew Moore for 'In as a Lion, Out as a Lamb'
Candace Kubinec for 'Revenant'
Hannah van Didden for 'The Wife'
Jade Williams for 'Dying to Travel'
Soramimi Hanarejima for 'Attention Management'
Steven Simoncic for 'You Will Do This'

Cadence Mandybura's fiction has been published in FreeFall, NōD, Fudoki Magazine, *and the* Bacopa Literary Review. *When she isn't writing, Cadence practises martial arts and plays Japanese taiko drums. Learn more at cadencemandybura.com.*

Laura Kuhlmann is a Romanian scientist and emerging writer currently based in Toronto. Her short stories and flash fiction have been published online and in print by Reflex Fiction *and* Semiahmoo Art Society, *and in the Carrick Publishing anthology* A Grave Diagnosis. *Laura is currently editing her first novel.*

The Weeping Pools

by Cadence Mandybura

Sister Margaret needed to find out where the children were going at night. She could have put a stop to it when she first noticed children slipping out of the lodge, but she was too curious to halt them just yet. If she understood where they were going, she would be better equipped to correct their behaviour. They were cunning about it, too: only a few went out each night, their empty beds camouflaged with heaped pillows that must have been donated by other children. Even in their truancy, they helped each other.

On the next clear night, Sister Margaret hid in a dark hollow of the chapel, where she had a good view of the lodge door. The cold kept her awake as she surveyed the silvery stillness of the forest, so different from her home country. She felt like she was trespassing into another world, with the edges and slopes of the landscape painted in chalky moonlight. They had made it through the worst of winter, but spring still seemed distant, a quiet rumour beneath the snow-dusted ground.

Over the course of an hour, she watched three small figures sneak out of the lodge. They all moved the same, taking a few stealthy steps away from the building before bursting into a run. After waiting long enough to determine that no more children were emerging, Sister Margaret began her pursuit. She was surprised to see that they had left their shoes behind, their tracks in the snow small curves with perfect toe-dots.

The tracks branched from the main trail to a thicket that Sister Margaret would have thought impassable. Cued by the footprints, she found her way past the branches with a crouch and pivot. A few steps farther and she began to hear high voices soaring in long, ghostly syllables. She continued in fear and excitement, wondering what ungodly rite she might catch the children in. The school strictly forbade any such barbaric practices, and Sister Margaret wondered if her discipline hadn't actually eradicated the customs, as she had hoped, but merely pushed them outside.

The trail wended through thick trunks then dipped, the spongy undergrowth shifting to stone. About twenty paces before her, the exposed rocks puckered around a dark pool that glinted with scraps of moonlight and exhaled thick curls of steam.

The children sat in a semicircle, holding hands, their pyjamas rolled up above skinny brown legs thrust into the hot spring. With her own toes freezing in spite of her boots, Sister Margaret could imagine how good the steaming water must feel after their barefoot sprint through the woods. She edged closer, trying to see their faces: there was Jonah, broad-faced and slow; Innocent, one of their youngest, doted upon by the more maternal girls; and was that sweet little Agnes?

They didn't notice her because they were weeping. Tear streaks gleamed on their dark cheeks, their eyes and lips shadowy crescents.

They were singing—the ghost syllables from earlier—a high unbroken aria of pain.

Sister Margaret didn't recognize them in their grief. Her children rarely cried, except when they first arrived at the school; even the boys cried sometimes when their hair was cut. A little strapping, early on, corrected the behaviour. If Sister Margaret had allowed herself to feel pride, she would have thought she had a deft hand with the children: not too heavy, not too light. But now, at this witching hour, where were her cheerful, dutiful children?

She walked towards them, not too fast. She didn't want them scattering into the forest with their poor wet feet.

"Children," she said, kind but firm. "You are not supposed to be out here."

As though she had broken a trance, the children's eyes came to life, flickering to find each other. They whispered urgently in the black gabble of their mother tongue before letting the words fade back into tears.

The heat venting from the pool warmed Sister Margaret's cheekbones as she got closer. "Come back to the lodge, now," she said. "You should be in bed."

She tried to meet their eyes—Jonah, Innocent, Agnes—but their liquid gazes wouldn't connect with hers. Jonah began wailing again, his voice thin and endless.

She stepped to the edge of the pool. None of the children moved. Would she have to carry the stubborn creatures back?

But now, so close to the water, she was curious. Ignoring the children for a moment, she knelt and reached a cold white hand to the water, telling herself she only wanted to find out how warm it was.

As her knuckles brushed the hot spring, a chasm tore through her heart — so violent and raw, she knew at once it was a wound that would never heal. Grief burned through her, bigger than her one small life, girded by a low, limitless ache.

She felt what the children were feeling; and, much worse, she felt how she had helped cause it.

From somewhere deeper than bone, beyond memory, Margaret began to weep. Her keening mingled with the children's, their sorrow rising with the steam to the stars.

River's Thousand-One Voice

BY CADENCE MANDYBURA

River is cold and chatters all day in her thousand-one voice. Big sister says that's not how you count, but I ask her how you say it when something is a thousand things and one thing at once, like River, and big sister has no answer.

I spend a lot of time with River. You can make little whirl-pools if you poke her in the right way, but I'm always more interested in her sounds than her shapes. She makes a medium *glug-a-lug* if you hold a branch underwater and let her bend around it, and a small *fipp* if you strike the surface instead.

Get a big rock and huck it—*kersploosh!* Everyone knows that one. Get a flat stone, pick your angle, wing it across the water's surface, and watch the rock hop. *Pad-pad-pad-pad-plop*, light as a cat's step until the river gulps the stone whole. Most people know that one, too.

Long after most kids get bored and run off to play their ball games, I keep testing out new sounds. A mittful of dirt, flung proper, makes a soft fizz over River's gabble. Gravel, on the other hand, makes a dense *pop-pop-pop-pop* that you can stretch, depending. Throw slow to give the sound a long tail.

For wedges, I like branches better than rocks, but either will do. A thick branch bundles River around it, with lots of possible results. Maybe you've broken a silky current, and now you have a choppy *splash-splash-splash* as the water jumps against stone. Or maybe you've smoothed a rough patch, taken away one swishy patter. Or you create a deep gurgle, maybe funny, and it can be sad or scary, too.

But it's okay to be sad or scared around River. Sometimes I step back and let her chatter, fast and cold, in her thousand-one voice. I can always rely on her.

Not like home. I can't predict the voices anymore. Big sister is getting quieter and quieter, and she's always looking past everything around her. Sometimes after angry noises, she comes and holds me and says nothing. But I can feel how she shakes.

She hasn't talked about running away, but I hear it in her long grey silences. I'm staying home more, afraid if I leave that big sister might be gone when I get back. I ask if she wants to visit River with me, but big sister says no. So I stop playing with River. Instead, I come straight home with big sister after school every day, and stick close when we do our chores and homework.

Now big sister is gone, and I visit River for the first time in a long while. But when I get there, I don't recognize River. I can't hear her thousand-one voice like I used to. She runs on in a hard rush. I'm cold, and I chatter.

Glimpse of a Goddess

by Laura Kuhlmann

I held you in my arms as the boat navigated the fjord through the heavy mist. Every time I picked you up, you got lighter. You couldn't get any lighter.

"Almost there," I whispered over the water.

The loud exhale of a whale startled me. How the giants sneak up on us — the killer whales in the water, the cancer in your blood. Could it be the same pod that had accompanied us to this little shrine west of Vancouver four weeks ago?

In front and to my right, the mountain rose: your island, perpetually covered by mist, the top crowned once again by wispy grey clouds.

"I brought you to your Goddess as I promised." I hugged you.

In my ears your voice still echoed off the cliff: "Can you see her nose, Mama?" You had pointed at the rock protruding sideways from the mountain. "The hair?" The clouds rolled heavy atop the rock. "There, by the water, is her waist. And the water is her skirt." I stared at the roiling water surrounding the pebbly shore, the foam spreading like lace atop the dark-green fabric of water.

The orcas smoothened the liquid silk with their backs, broke it and dove back. The water mended itself once they disappeared just below the surface.

It was the same pod: one mother and two calves. The Goddess of the island was hiding them in her skirt of water, just like last time.

"I can't get any closer," the captain yelled over the engine.

The orcas puffed as they circled our now-silent boat.

Rounded boulders jotted out of the bare slope of the mountain like old bones protruding through crumbling skin. My eyes clouded as I remembered your ribs protruding through your frail skin as the pain in your face dissolved away.

I opened the urn and scooped you out, then dipped you into the water. One fist at a time, I let you go, let you swim with the orcas around the Goddess of the island.

"Take good care of her," I asked the mountain, as the engine roared back to life.

BLUE SKIES OVER NINE ISLES

Joseph Stilwell &
Hugh Henderson

Joseph Stilwell *has slain gods, devoured galaxies, and sired several ruling dynasties. He is either the most powerful man in the multiverse or a very accomplished liar. See more of his lies @animisticengine on Twitter.*

Hugh Henderson *is a Vancouver-based artist, creating everything from magical Dungeons & Dragons items to pirate-ship planes with flame throwers! You can find full-colour pages of his comic at blueskiescomic. com, and see more of his art at patreon.com/hughhenderson.*

TARGET AHEAD.

WE HAVE VISUAL.
THAT'S A LOT OF BOGEYS...

JUST MEANS A LOT OF GLORY, MANTIS. CANNONS HOT.

MAXWELL ROMERO.
WHAT--?

THESE THINGS ARE FAST!
MAGPIE, WATCH YOUR SEVEN!
TOO MANY! CAN'T GET CLEAR!
THEY'RE ON MY WING! SOMEONE
WHOEVER'S LEFT, FORM UP ON ME!
YOU WILL BE PROCESSED.

NNNHII
PATROSA SPIERA.
SNRRK

NOTIFICATION
NEW MESSAGE
WHAT'S THIS?

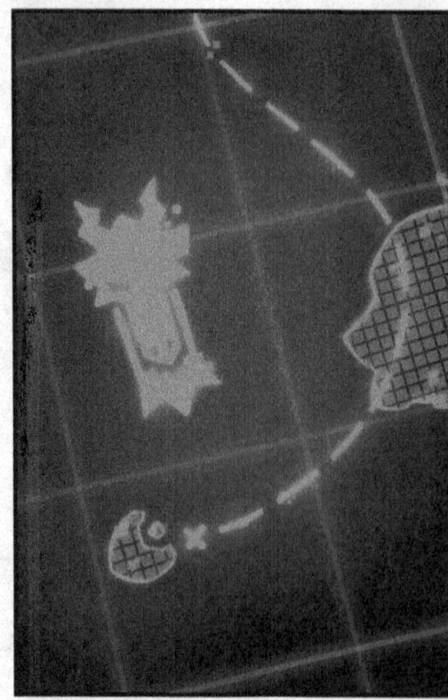

HUH?
TEN EXTRA HOURS?

WHATEVER.

MORNING!
GET ENOUGH SHUT EYE?
SURE DID.

WAIT.

WHY DIDN'T YOU FOLLOW MY ROUTE?
IT ADDED 10 HOURS.

TO AVOID PIRATE WATERS!
IS THAT WHAT THE DRAGON MEANT?
HUH.
I'M GONNA DIE WITHOUT EVEN SEEING AMBER CITY!
RELAX, THE RADAR WILL DETECT ANYTHING BEFORE--
PA PAPA PING
WHAT?

BLUE SKIES
Over Nine Isles

CHRONICLER:
JOSEPH STILWELL

CARTOGRAPHER:
HUGH HENDERSON

WRONG
-URP-
WAY!
THEY'VE GOT ME PENNED IN!
AND DON'T PUKE IN MY PLANE!
SCARTO! THEY'RE GOOD...
DON'T ADMIRE THEM!
-GULP-
THUNK
WHATAREYOUDOING
WHATAREYOUDOING!?

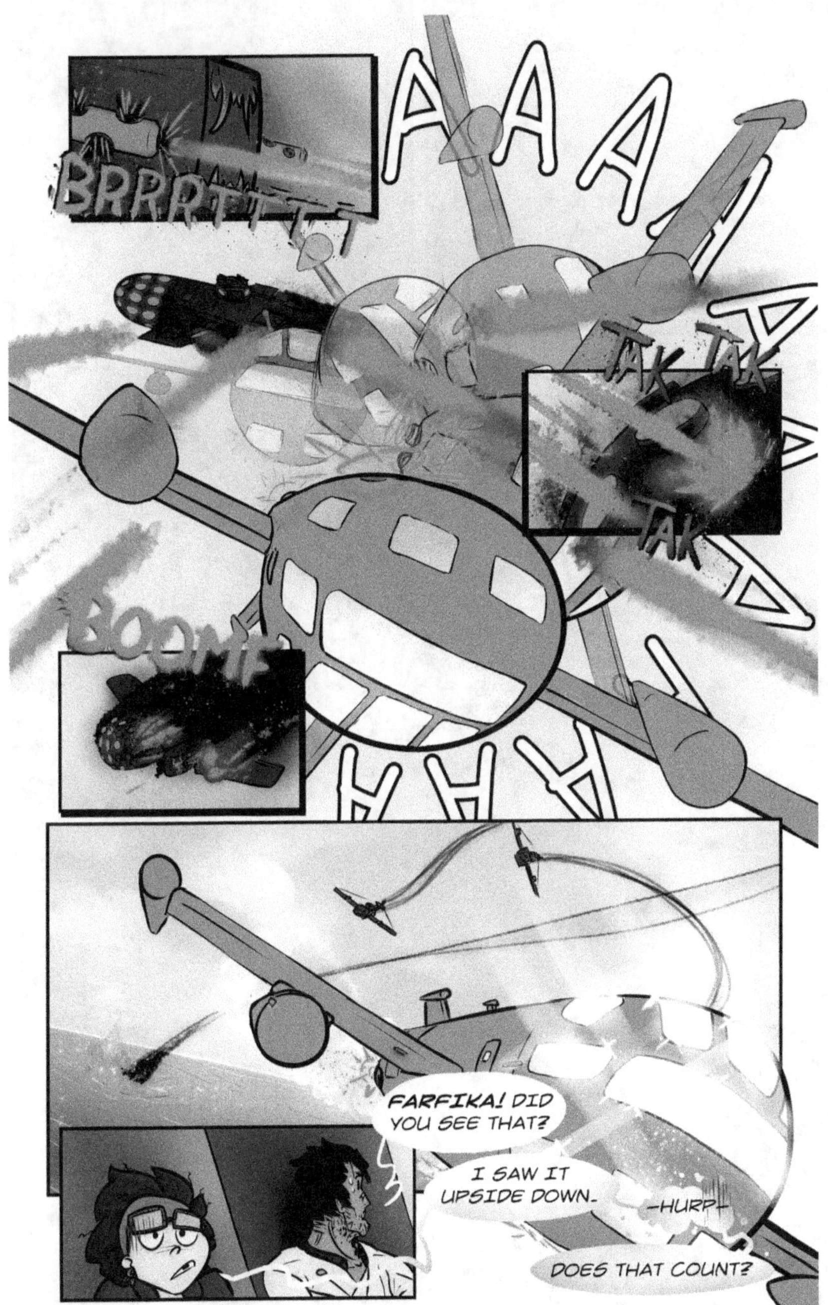

BRRRTTTT
AAAA
A
TAK TAK
TAK
BOOM
AAAA
FARFIKA! DID YOU SEE THAT?
I SAW IT UPSIDE DOWN.
—HURP—
DOES THAT COUNT?

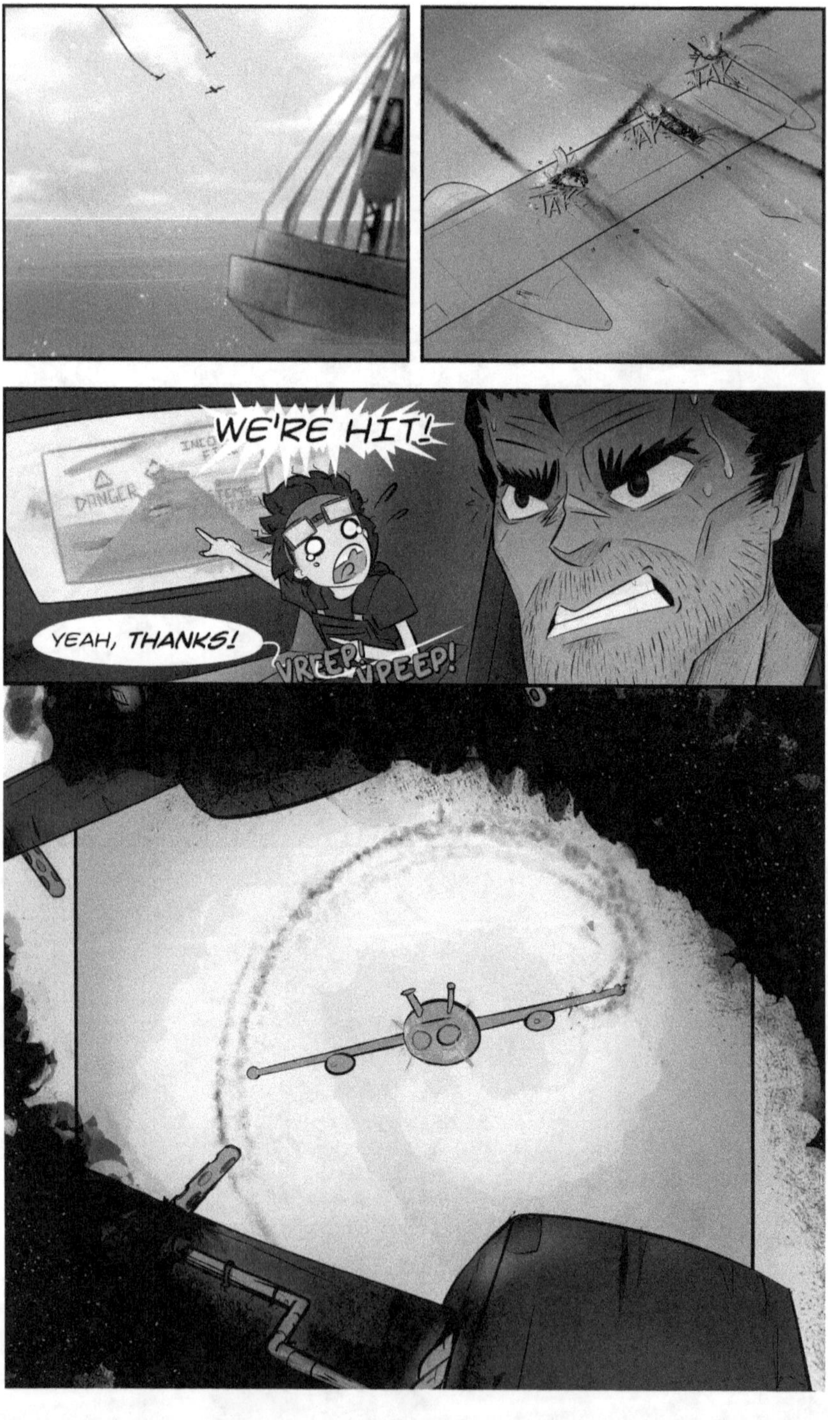

WE'RE HIT!
DANGER
YEAH, THANKS!
VREEP! VREEP!

SHRAK-
-A-BOOM!!

ESH BUA!
WE'RE GONNA LIVE!
DEET DEET!

THIS IS CAPTAIN SARA BEHARI OF THE NINE ISLES DEFENSE FORCE.
EVERYTHING ALRIGHT?
YES! THANK YOU, CAPTAIN.
THINK NOTHING OF IT, MR...?
MAXWELL ROMERO.
AND I'M MARLOW DREYFUSS!

WELL, MR. ROMERO AND MS. DREYFUSS, IF YOU JUST TRANSMIT YOUR CODES, YOU CAN BE ON YOUR WAY.
OF COURSE, ONE SECOND!

COMMUNICATION CLOSED
WHAT CODES?

YOUR FLIGHT CODES AND DOCKING ID, DUH. EVERY PLANE HERE'S GOT 'EM.
COMMUNICATION CLOSED
MARLOW. MY PLANE ISN'T FROM HERE.

OH, RIGHT.

UH.

SCRAP.

CAPTAIN—
DREET-DREET!
OUR CODES GOT STOLEN!
NO, THEY DIDN'T—
I DON'T HAVE TIME FOR GAMES. PRODUCE YOUR CODES OR BE TREATED AS HOSTILE.
WAIT! I'M NOT FROM AROUND HERE! THAT'S WHY I HAVE NO CODES!
WE DON'T GET MANY FOREIGNERS HERE...
IF YOU'LL COME WITH US, WE CAN SORT THIS OUT.

OF COURSE! WE DON'T WANT ANY TROUBLE...
TRANSMITTING FLIGHT PATH. PLEASE FOLLOW IT EXACTLY.

YEAH, HE'S REAL GOOD AT THAT
UNDERSTOOD.
WHAT ARE——

LOOK!
IS THAT...
AMBER CITY!

OK, I'M IMPRESSED.
IT'S JUST LIKE THE PICTURES!

LOOK! THERE'S SHANTY POINT! THE ORIGINAL SETTLEMENT!
THAT LITTLE SCRAP HEAP?

AND THERE'S THE GRAND DOCKS!

WE MUST BE GETTING CLOSE
TO WHAT?
THERE!

THE CHARTER'S GUILD!
CHARTERS GUILD
CHARTERS GUILD
CURTIS, GET READY.
WE HAVE BUSINESS WITH THE NIDF.
I CAN GUESS WHAT THAT IS...

MAX
I DON'T LIKE THIS...
RELAX. WE HAVE NOTHING TO HIDE.

YOU DON'T KNOW THE NIDF.
AND YOU DO?

I'VE HEARD STORIES!

LOOK, THEY COULD HAVE VAPED US, BUT THEY DIDN'T.
THAT'S A GOOD--
KRRUNK
WHAT WAS THAT?
NOTHING GOOD!
NO, WAIT!
THEY PROBABLY JUST WANT TO--
HATCH OPEN
--TALK.

MAXWELL RAMERO.
I AM CAPTAIN BEHARI.
SHOW US YOUR HANDS
AND EXIT YOUR VESSEL.

WHAT BROUGHT YOU TO THE NINE ISLES?
JUST PASSING--
NONE OF YOUR BUSINESS!

WE'LL HAVE TO SEARCH YOUR VESSEL.
NO WAY!
OF COURSE.

What is this? Crank-tech?
Too advanced. Maybe Two-Spear.
MAX! WHAT ARE YOU DOING?
COOPERATING.

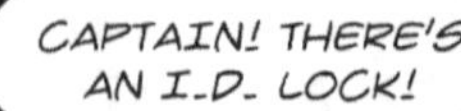

CAPTAIN! THERE'S AN I.D. LOCK!

OPEN IT.
CERTAINLY.
MAX, NO.
IT'S FINE, MARLOW.
WE HAVE...

...NOTHING TO HIDE.

CONFISCATE THAT ILLEGAL SALVAGE.
HOW CAN SALVAGE BE ILLEGAL?
HE REALLY ISN'T FROM HERE, IS HE?
NOPE.
I'M GUESSING YOU DON'T HAVE A SALVAGE PERMIT.

HOW MANY PERMITS ARE THERE?
DO I NEED A PERMIT TO TAKE A NAP?

DRAMATICS WON'T HELP.
WHY? DO I NEED A DRAMA LICENSE?

WE ARE IMPOUNDING YOUR VESSEL UNTIL FURTHER NOTICE.
WHAT?!
NO!

WE'LL NEED TO QUESTION YOU BEFORE——
CAPTAIN
WAIT

THIS PLANE IS MY HOME.
I HAVE NOWHERE TO GO WITHOUT IT.

DON'T WORRY, WE HAVE TEMPORARY ACCOMMODATION.

I CAN'T BELIEVE YOU DIDN'T KNOW ABOUT SALVAGE PERMITS.
WE SPLIT THE TROUBLE 50/50 TOO.
SO WE ARE PARTNERS?
PUKABOD.*
*EXPLETIVE

ALLAIGNA'S SONG: OBURAKOR

JM Landels

JM Landels *is torn between travelling the world to teach writing and swordfighting, and never leaving her idyllic farm in Langley, BC. Her debut series, fantasy bestseller* Allaigna's Song: Overture, *and the sequel,* Aria, *are available from Pulp Literature Press and Amazon. You can follow her adventures with pen and sword at jmlandels.stiffbunnies.com. In this issue we present the second part of the novella* Allaigna's Song: Oburakor, *which is set between the second and third novels of the trilogy. If you missed the first part, catch it in* Pulp Literature *Issue 27, Summer 2020.*

Previously in *Allaigna's Song: Oburakor* . . .

*After six years in the Brandishear Rangers, Allaigna has mustered out. Upon
leaving, she receives a mysterious note from her grandfather offering her a private
commission. The task takes her and a handful of mercenaries to an unknown
wasteland. One of the company is her cousin Goffree, who seems not to have
recognized her yet. With a sandstorm on the horizon, however, family reunions
will have to wait.*

Verse 3

The Killing Ground

It was a good ten minutes of forced jog before the smudge
resolved into the shape of a building, and another five before
it was evident the building was ruined. We slowed, all of us
breathing hard by now and coughing on the dust-filled air.

It was a keep—a single square tower, half the height it must
once have been. No doubt its roof and floors were long since
gone, but at least it had walls.

If the wind had been blowing the other way, if our noses
hadn't been clogged with dust, we probably would have smelled
it first. Instead it was the Ilvani woman who stumbled into the
mouth of the keep then reeled back into us, gagging.

The light was failing as the sand closed in and the sun sank lower, but there was just enough of it to reveal the gruesome sight within. The square enclosure was drenched in blackened blood, from the four walls to the broken stone floor to the bodies—and parts of bodies—strewn about like so much unwashed laundry. Flies, safe from the wind, made their own counterpart to the howling sand outside. It was all I could do to not vomit on the spot, and I held my hand over my mouth, retching as I scanned the ramparts from the doorway.

The ruined walls seemed to hold no obvious threats. I looked at Redbeard, who'd reached my side in the doorway a second after me, and then at Goff on my other side. I could see the same question in each of their eyes: whether to take shelter in the scene of this massacre, not knowing what caused it—and if its author was still around—or whether to continue to flee the sand storm in hope of finding an alternative?

It pleased me to see that the short-haired woman had moved left and was stringing her small bow as she peered around the outside corner of the building. The Chriani lookalike was doing the same to the right. Well trained, these ones, whoever they were.

Hand still over my mouth, I motioned Goff to follow the woman and circle to the far side to check for threats. He and I both had trained with Brandishear forces, and he knew the signals common between Rangers and Knights. But would he take orders from me?

He did, not questioning except for the back-of-the-mind look his eyes hadn't lost since we met. I motioned for the Ilvani woman to take the right, wondering if she would comprehend. But it seemed she knew more than the average Ilvani of our military protocol. I couldn't worry about that now.

I motioned Redbeard and we stepped through the door. I didn't string my bow, wanting instead to have a sword in hand. We circled away from each other, stepping carefully over the carnage. When we converged again by the far wall and nothing had moved except the flies, we met each other's eyes. With unspoken assent, we began picking our way amongst the bodies to see if any of them were whole enough to have a chance of being alive.

None that I saw were; but I began to notice details of their armour, faces, and build. These men — and men they all were — were huge. Not so much tall as broad, their clean-shaven jaws attached to necks like tree trunks. Each of them looked like more than a match for the heaviest prize wrestler in the Ilmar, and yet they had been slaughtered, dismembered, and scattered about this keep like so many discarded dolls.

Essaruk. Barbarians from Oburakor across the eastern mountains. A nation with whom we were at peace, only by dint of the fact the mountain passes were too hard to get armies through. What were they doing here in Brandishear? The cold reminder that I still had no idea where I was or what was going on was interrupted by a moan.

I snapped my head around to see Redbeard crouching by a body. I helped him roll a bloodied corpse, massively heavy despite a missing leg, off of the smaller body below.

This was a woman in some sort of ceremonial robe, her hair and throat adorned with hammered brass jewellery and beads. She was breathing, but barely, and her dark eyelids fluttered in her striking, square-chinned face when Redbeard put a hand beside her neck to check her pulse.

Goff walked in at that moment, followed by the Ilvani.

He coughed, spat sand from his mouth. "All clear round the perimeter. Harthor and Olenbry are doing another sweep."

I filed the names away to sort out whose face was whose later.

"This one's alive," Redbeard told no one in particular. "But perhaps not for long."

He took a canteen from his pack and dribbled a bit of water into the Essaruk woman's mouth. She coughed and spat it back up along with blood.

I'd been watching Goff and the Ilvani take in our surroundings. The former seemed appalled enough at the bloodshed but unsurprised by the identity of the victims. The Ilvani, her hand still over her face from the smell, scowled and muttered something that could only be a curse. She kicked at one of the corpses then spat on it. Ilvani love Essaruk even less than they like us Ilmari. But through the vehemence, I could see fear in her eyes. She, too, was wondering how they got here.

Redbeard snapped a glance in her direction and growled at her in Ilvanin. "Show respect for the dead, woman."

"*Entarren,*" she prefaced her reply. "Stop wasting water on that *fildhradh.*"

"Stand down," said Goff, putting a hand on her shoulder. She shrugged it off.

The Woodkin seemed to have better doctoring skills than I with my field first aid, so I left the Essaruk woman to him and stepped over two fallen bodies to reach Goff's side.

"What did you see outside?"

"Nothing." If he had recognized me yet, he still didn't show it.

"Nothing? No tracks? A force large enough to kill this many warriors would have at least left traces, even in this wind."

He shook his head. "Whatever killed them might as well have descended from the sky."

The Ilvani woman's eyes were wide, her nostrils distended like a frightened horse's, but her voice was calm. "There are no tracks of these *Entarren* arriving either. The wind has taken care of all that."

That made some sense, of course, but it was an uneasy sort of sense. With no tracks to or from this place, we had no idea who had slaughtered the Essaruk, where they had gone, or how far away they might be.

I bent over the nearest corpse, removed my glove, and reluctantly felt his face, the back of his neck, and the skin beneath his tooled-leather breastplate.

I could be dispassionate when I needed to be. "He's only just cooling off," I said, and I pointed to the pools of blood on the broken stones and the dirt of the keep floor. "And much of that is still red. They haven't been dead more than a bell—two at most."

The sound that had been missing suddenly filtered in as crows began settling on the broken walls of the keep, hunching down against the buffeting wind and sand but unwilling yet to join us on the ground. It was the first sign of life other than the woman and the flies, and I welcomed their presence, morbid as it was.

"Even the *moradhen* are just arriving," the Ilvani pointed out.

I nodded, though some niggling thing sat at the back of my mind.

I looked at Goff, waiting for him to take leadership or at least offer some explanation. But he looked at least as confused as the rest of us.

"Well," I said at last, "I don't think we have many choices but to wait out the storm here. We can at least move these bodies to one corner, though." When neither of them moved, but stood there with their panicked eyes flicking to the battlements, I added, "I can't lift these brutes myself." That snapped Goff out of it. He grabbed the body by the shoulders while I lifted the legs. Even divided, the dead weight was staggering.

"Rennielle," he said to the Ilvani. "Spell one of those two on watch." She nodded, evidently relieved not to have to sully her hands on an Essaruk carcass.

Goff and I had just managed to shift the first body over against the wall when the thought that had been bothering me made itself clear. The crows had just appeared, the bodies were still warm, and yet the flies and putrid smell spoke of things long dead.

"Olenbry," Goff called as the short-haired woman came back into the keep, unwinding the scarf from around her face and shaking sand from it, "help us with these."

As we moved another body, Olenbry let out a muffled yelp of surprise and suppressed a sudden gag. The smell washed over us. Beneath the freshly dead corpse was another that had been that way much longer. Whether it was Essaruk, Ilmari, or Ilvani was impossible to tell, for the features and much of the flesh had long since been carried off by crows. Worse, though, were the stakes to which the victim's limbs were tied, leaving him spread-eagled in the centre of the ruined stone floor.

Unable to suppress it any longer, I dropped the leg of the Essaruk I carried, and vomited on the blood-soaked ground.

It seemed to take forever, though I'm sure it was less than a bell before Goff, Olenbry, and I had laid out the dead Essaruk in one corner of the keep. None of us wanted to tackle the other body — the one that seemed to have been tortured … or sacrificed.

Feeling stained and sickened by the undertaker's job we'd just performed, I crossed to where Redbeard now had the Essaruk woman wrapped in his cloak, her head propped on his pack. I envied him the job of tending to the living.

I squatted beside him. "Will she live?"

"I'm not sure." I was struck again by his mellifluous voice. "She has very little blood left within her—I'm surprised she's alive at all. The eastern tribes are said to be a hardy race. I'd thought that was just rumour till now." It was the largest continuous set of words I'd heard from my new companions. And I shivered again. How little I knew of the people I had to now put my trust in. This man, though, had compassion in his voice, and I decided on my first point of alliance.

"I'm Allaigna," I said, extending my hand. He met it, palm to palm, in the Woodkin greeting.

"Imerian," he said. "Of Tillhartha." I was startled. Tillhartha was another name for the Eastern Forest, whose edge bordered my once-home of Teillai.

I would have said more, but Goff and Olenbry came over at that moment. Goff turned to the short woman. "Fetch the others. We need to talk."

Her eyes flashed as if she weren't used to taking orders, or at least not from him, but she went anyway.

"Allaigna," he said. "That's a name from the past."

I stood, brushing sand and filth from my hands, and faced him. We were of a height now, and I could look him straight in the eye—something I never came close to when I was twelve and he fourteen.

"It's good to see you again, Goff," I said, and realized, the situation notwithstanding, it was true.

"When did you recognize me?" he asked.

I smiled for the first time in that extended day. "When I walked into the room."

He shook his head. "I'm an idiot."

"That," I said, "has always been so. But in your defence, I have grown considerably."

He nodded, looked me up and down with an eye that made me blush like a twelve-year-old all over again. "Well, there's no one I'd rather have at my side, cuz," he said. He wrapped me in a brief hug, stepping away before Olenbry and the others walked in.

"Besides," he added, patting the sword hanging at my hip. "You still owe a blow on my behalf with that."

Harthor, the thin, dark-haired man who looked so much like Chriani, came in last. He glanced around the keep, took in the gruesome tidying job we'd done, and switched his flickering, watchful gaze to the walls. He scowled, shaking sand out of his hair. "You think it's wise to leave the perimeter unwatched?"

"Just for a while," Goff said. "We need all our heads in the circle for now."

Imerian spoke up again. "Anything out there that hasn't taken cover by now will be buried soon."

There was a collective shudder at this as we all looked at the darkened, howling sky, the sand streaking past the doorway that, to our good fortune, opened leeward. And then we all turned to Goff.

"Where are we?" I asked. "And what happened here?"

I sat down on the other side of the convalescent woman and looked up at Goff while the others settled in a circle around him like a gaggle of children waiting for a story.

"First things first." He cleared his throat. "We need to set up a watch, prepare to defend ourselves——"

"No," I interrupted, "first you need to tell us where in the seven hells we are and how we got here."

The Ilvani opened her mouth, no doubt to argue, but I continued. "As Imerian here says, there's not much that will come at us through that storm." I glanced at the crows, who were stationed on the buttresses of the missing floor above us, hunkered down against the wind. "Even the scavengers are waiting." I repeated my question, expanding it. "Where are we, and why?"

"Oburakor," he said.

Rennielle was back on her feet with sword drawn. "Liar," she spat, levelling the tip of the sword at Goff's chest. "That is impossible."

Goff raised a hand and pushed the sword aside as if it were no more than a branch in his path.

"You're sworn to harm none of us, Rennielle. Look around you. Where else might we be?"

"What sorcery brought us here, at least four hundred leagues east?" Her face was twitching, expressions of anger and fear chasing one another across it.

"The awesome energy needed to transport six of us, *alive*," Harthor said, pausing as with the weight of wonder in his face, "is something no mage has been able to summon since before the Cataclysm." His pale eyes bored through Goff. "You'd best tell us all you know, sir. For none of us have sworn the oath she has."

He left the threat hanging in the air between them. I could see Goff bristle for a moment, and then the familiar smooth mask slid back over his face. "Indeed, I do owe you all an explanation." He gave a slight smile, a gesture so out of place but so charming, even here, I could feel the tension in the circle slacken ever so slightly.

"The Mageguard has been working to restore the lothgates."

I had heard of lothgates, used by the Imperial Guard, the Lotherasien, before the Cataclysm. The gates, powered by massive arcane sources unknown to us now, had allowed the Lotherasien to maintain control over an empire that stretched well beyond the boundaries of the Ilmar. Many believed the use of the gates themselves had somehow caused the Cataclysm in Ulaonnor-Mor. And the Mageguard was trying to restore them? I would have liked to think my grandfather knew nothing of this. But he had sent me here. I shivered.

"Never mind how," I snapped. "Why? Why us, why here?"

Goff turned to me, his eyes pondering. "Early scouting missions indicated this one was still partially active. Able to receive, if not send."

Olenbry interrupted. "And they sent *six people* here as a test? Are our lives worth that little?"

"Would you send a single person, or even two or three, into *this?*" He looked around the circle at us. "You all have … debts … to the throne, or you wouldn't be here." I could tell by the way his gaze travelled that all these people had secrets, and he was party to them. "Except you." His eyes fell on me. "I didn't know you were to be included."

Neither did I. I wondered what I'd done to deserve this punishment from my grandfather.

Imerian broke our locked stares. "We have supplies, I take it?" He pointed to the identical packs everyone carried but me. "There is enough dry brush here for a small fire. I think we could all use revictualizing."

I nodded. "I'll keep first watch by the door," I said.

I stationed myself in the lee of the wind, watching the crows and sorting the disturbing thoughts that had invaded my head.

Verse 4

Solace in the Desert

The light was almost entirely gone now. I could no longer see the sand whipping horizontally past the keep's doorway; I could only hear its scouring screech against stone walls, punctuated by staccato bursts of pebbles and dry bits of desert brush joining in. Though I was theoretically keeping watch, there was nothing I could watch other than the flickering darkness. My eyes turned instead to the centre of the keep, where Imerian had built a meagre fire from the few bits of dried brush we could find. I could tell from the arcane light it cast he was using Woodkin magic to prolong its life and increase its heat. A useful talent, but I hoped he would not exhaust himself using it. I knew a similar charm, but my lifelong habit of hiding my Leisanmira magic was deeply ingrained, and I was reluctant to let these strangers know of it. Also, I couldn't help but think it was wise to keep my reserves of strength in case I needed them later.

Though the firelight was dim, it was enough for my eyes. I was even less comfortable with the measure of Ilvani blood in my veins than I was with my gipsy heritage, but I couldn't deny the sharper senses that came with it were useful.

From my pocket I retrieved the sweaty note. It was hard to believe a mere day had passed since I'd been given it. I unfolded it, read it again, trying desperately to find the reason my grandfather had sent me into this perfidious trap. Did he not know? I wanted to believe that, but couldn't. A small part of me hoped his actions were a measure of trust — that he'd sent me on a vital mission because of his faith in my abilities. But if that were the case, why didn't he tell me more? I put that note away before my eyes watered more than could be accounted for by the wind.

All the others except Imerian had laid themselves out to rest on what packs and clothes they had. The Woodkin was tending the still-unconscious Essaruk, but as I watched, he rose and walked over.

"How is she?" I asked.

"No better, possibly worse," he replied. "What about you?"

I gave a sandy laugh. "The same, I'd say."

He crouched beside me and held out an open palm. On it sat a single withered hawberry. I squinted, shifting my sight into the magical realm to reveal the pinkish glow around it.

"Thanks, but I don't think a single dried berry will do much for my empty stomach," I said. "I'm too parched to swallow at the moment."

He made an impatient sound. "It's not poison, you know."

"I can tell that. I'm a ranger." That, at least, was information I was willing to share.

He ignored me. "It is be-spelled, though. We grow these specifically for their healing properties."

I raised an eyebrow. Angeley had bought them from tree-priests before — though they seldom traded them at fairs. "I'm not sick or injured."

He shrugged. "Or tired? Hungry? Aching? The others have all had one."

I reached out and put my hands on his, closing his fingers around the berry. It was our first moment of physical contact, and I was surprised by how welcome it felt to have my skin against the warm rough hands of another.

"Save it," I said. "Who knows when we might need it more?"

He shrugged and put it back in a linen bag.

"Do you want company while you keep watch?" he asked.

I did, I realized, desperately. But I also needed more time to think.

I shook my head. "I'm fine. Get some sleep." As he rose, I added, "But thank you."

He inclined his head, his face invisible now in the darkness. "I'll relieve you at mid-moon," he said.

I looked up at the black, storm-covered sky, wondering how he expected me to tell when it was mid-moon. Woodkin had a far better sense of time than even those of us who slept in the woods for a living.

"I'll wake you in two bells," I replied, contrary in my use of city terms.

"No need," he said. "I'll be up." He walked away before I could get the last word in.

It was less than two bells, however, when I was alerted by a sound near the fire: a low moan or grunt, followed by a cough.

I rose, shook the accumulated sand from my coat, and moved toward the dying fire, stepping around the prostrate forms of my companions. They were light sleepers all, and by the time I reached the side of the Essaruk woman, there was too much motion around me to listen properly.

"Hst!" I shushed them, and, like well-trained soldiers, they froze. In the dim glow of the fire I motioned Imerian over, and together we checked the pulse and breath of the woman. Her eyes fluttered, and she coughed once more, froth appearing at her lips followed by a trickle of darker liquid.

It was a bad sign. I helped Imerian roll her onto her side, fully aware we could be making the damage to her lungs worse but unable to prevent her from choking any other way.

She whimpered in pain.

Imerian bundled a cloak behind her and used his handkerchief to wipe the blood and froth from her face.

"Can you hear me?" he asked, and was answered by a moan and flutter of the eyes.

"I'd say she does," I responded. "But she may not speak our tongue."

I moved around to face her, my head down low to hear. Her eyes spread more, and I waved two fingers in front of her face. "Do you speak Ilmarin?" I asked, and was greeted by a blank, confused look. "What about Ilvanin?" I asked in that language. The eyes focussed, becoming harder.

"No matter," came Rennielle's voice from behind me. "I speak Sarukken."

I looked at the Ilvani woman. Not the best choice of translator, since she was the one who'd advocated letting the Essaruk die. But no one else came forward. She didn't crowd beside me but stood, towering over us, and spoke in a voice as cutting as the wind that howled overhead.

"*Ik'tak gven.*"

The woman on the ground winced as she replied, as if forcing air between her lips cost her. "*Hash-ten'al.*"

Goff came to stand beside Rennielle. "Ask her what happened here."

"She can barely speak," I interrupted. "How about starting with her name?"

Rennielle looked at me with unmasked contempt. "She won't live past dawn with that chest wound. Her name hardly matters."

"Trokhagh. Name Trokhagh," the woman choked out in Ilmarin.

Goff and I exchanged a raised eyebrow. The other two had gathered near, their shadows further obscuring the woman's face.

"Trokhagh," Imerian said, his hand on her shoulder. "Nod if you understand me."

She did, her eyes wary.

"I'm going to give you something to chew. It will help the pain. Do you understand?"

She nodded again and Imerian placed the berry—the one I had refused—between her lips.

Rennielle strangled a cry and lurched forward, too late to stop him.

"*You stupid sack of vulture shit,*" she spat in Ilvanin before switching back to our tongue. "Squandering your magic on a dying *Githraki*."

Imerian was calm in his reply. "Dying is bad enough," he said. "Why would I let anyone die in pain if I could help it?"

He offered the Essaruk a sip of water to wash down the dried morsel.

"She'll be better able to answer you now, I think."

Goff crouched at last beside me and repeated his question.

"What happened here?"

She replied in Essaruk, and Rennielle ground out the story in Ilmarin.

The band of warriors we saw dead in here was her congregation. She was the mouthpiece of the strange gods worshipped by these barbarians, and she had led the band here to rest for the night on their pilgrimage to somewhere—a temple, the name of which was meaningless to us. They were attacked—and here the story made little sense—by warriors that appeared in their midst and disappeared as quickly.

Goff looked thoughtful. "Describe them," he said.

Rennielle had trouble with that translation. Their adjectives were not analogous to ours, but the word "lothar" came through. Goff paced, his thoughts his own, and we all watched him in the shrieking silence of the wind. Then she began speaking again. Rennielle glanced at her, a growing look of anger on her face.

Goff looked between them. "Well?" he snapped.

"She's hallucinating," Rennielle told him. "Insane."

He growled. "Just do the job you were hired for. Translate."

Her eyes narrowed and nostrils widened as she pronounced slowly, "She describes a man—no, a creature—with them. With eyes of flame, eight feet tall. And wings." She shrugged. "It is religious delirium. That is one of their heathen gods."

We were all fully awake now, restless like fowl that have seen a fox in the yard and will not settle.

Goff questioned the Essaruk woman more, about the locale, her tribe, her following, and their reason for straying so far from their home. The answers were important, I knew, but I found it hard to focus between the zinging of the sandstorm overhead and the overlapping voices as Rennielle translated.

The Essaruk's burst of lucidity wore off quickly, and she began to lose consciousness again. Imerian made her as comfortable as he could, but I could tell from the look on his face that he shared Rennielle's assessment: the woman would not live long.

I plucked at Goff's elbow. "We should talk." I motioned to a pile of fallen masonry in the far corner of the keep. "Alone," I added as the Ilvani started to follow us. She gave me a cool look with poison below it, but no matter. This was family business.

"Time you told me what's going on, Goff. There's more to this than a philosophical interest in lothgates."

He took a deep breath and ran a hand through his sand-filled dark curls.

"It seems the Essaruk have been able to reactivate a gate."

My mind whirled. Essaruk were known to have limited magic of the kind used by healers and tree-priests. Nothing that could power an arcane device of that magnitude. But my first question wasn't how.

"Where?" I asked.

"Holc," he replied, and my held breath eased out, but only one notch. At least it wasn't Aerach, or Brandishear. But Holc was still too close for comfort.

"A ranger patrol found a band of six Essaruk scouts half a day's march from Radhaven."

"Scouts?"

"Warriors. Not an emissary or clerk among them. The ranger troop lost half their number capturing two of them."

"And the rest?"

"Dead."

So the scouting mission failed at least. "And the captives?"

"At Adamiel's court."

I doubted they were guests there. The sickening presentiment loomed over me. Our peace with Oburakor was due largely to the fact the few mountain passes between it and the Ilmar were sealed and well guarded. But lothgates would change all that.

"So that's why Grandpapa needs them," I murmured, more to myself than anything. "But why us?"

Goff's face had hardened. "Grandpapa?" he repeated. "I had no idea you were on such cosy terms with him."

The wave of resentment I felt from him was chilling.

"Not anymore," I qualified. "Aside from him sending me here, we haven't spoken in years. And he has never publicly acknowledged me."

"Nor me," Goff said. "In public or private."

The bitterness I'd sensed at Goff's birthfeast so many years ago had grown no less.

"Why us?" I asked again. "Why two of his family on this suicidal task?"

"I think," he said slowly, "in some strange way he only trusts family. And also …" He paused, then released the bitter nut he'd been chewing. "He'd not be heartbroken to see two contenders to the throne gone."

"Contender?" I laughed, brushing off the disturbing thought. "Hardly. My mother was clearly stricken from the line when she was married."

There was a silence as we sat in our own thoughts. Could it be? Had Chanist Brandis seen me as a threat to his other children's lines? And how could I have been so naïve as to never see it?

"Do you think," I asked, pushing uncomfortable thoughts about my own heritage aside, "as Girondrey's grandson, your claim could pre-empt even his?"

"I make no claim," he said, but the emphasis on the last word made me wonder. Had his grandmother Taerysh raised him with hopes? "It takes a motion of the lords to elect a bastard to the throne."

"But it has happened." Brandis's granddaughter, I remembered from the lays, had birthed a child by an unknown father, and that child had ruled Brandishear for thirty years.

"Not in the last three hundred years," he replied.

So he had been thinking of it. I shrugged. I didn't want to encourage him. Goff would make a terrible prince. But he was family, and here in this wilderness that was all I had.

I smiled. "If I had my grandmother's gift for telling fortunes, I'd let you know if that changes."

His face hardened again. I remembered too late it was Nourd, another gipsy fortune teller, who had triggered the rift between us. Struggling for recovery, I slipped my arm in his and offered a piece of information I hadn't yet shared.

"At any rate, I'm glad to have found you again. We Brandis bastards need to stick together."

"Bastard? You?"

I nodded, let the pain I'd nearly forgotten resurface, and told him part of the reason I'd left home six years ago.

Verse 5

Magic in the Temple

The sandstorm faded at last in the grey hours of early morning, just as Imerian woke us from uneasy sleep. The wind had changed during the night, driving the last of the storm through the open door of the keep. It lay over us and the bodies of the dead like a dusting of early winter snow. We coughed, shimmied ourselves like horses after a roll, and began shaking sand out of our clothes and belongings.

The Essaruk woman had died in the night. If Imerian had noticed at the time, he hadn't woken us. But, I noted, her eyes were closed. Without comment, we moved her body to join those of her comrades.

The first rays of sun were stained crimson from the retreating storm and cast a bloody hue over the scene in mockery of the real blood that had dried, blackened, and been sipped up by sand overnight. Hardly a word was said as we packed up our makeshift camp, all of us relieved, no doubt, to busy our hands instead of our worries.

At last I turned to Goff. "So," I said, pausing longer than I thought necessary to give him a chance to take charge. "How do we get back?"

He wiped a gritty hand over his grittier face, and the expression that emerged on the other side was smooth and calm once more.

"South and west," he replied, pulling a leather tube out of his pack.

It contained a map, which he spread on the ground, holding it down with his knees and hands against the little gusts of wind that still danced through the keep.

The map was good quality and looked to be the work of royal cartographers, but it was incomplete. The western edges, which showed the borders of Holc and Aerach, were detailed, as were a few clumps of the larger Oburakor settlements. But there were vast stretches of emptiness.

As Goff smoothed it with his bare hand, he whispered something

I was not attentive enough to hear, and more lines began to appear on the chart. I moved my vision to the arcane spectrum and saw a bluish glow from the plain iron ring on his index finger spread and trickle across the map like a river flooding its banks. The newly visible lines were rougher, with some crabbed notes, marginalia and sketched diagrams. Expeditions into Oburakor had been going on for some time, it seemed. I was so engrossed I almost missed what Goff was saying.

"… here"—his finger pointed to a mark surrounded by notes—"is where we think the scouting party came from. It's an abandoned temple, but our scryers have detected more activity here lately. If so, that lothgate should take us back to Holc."

"*If* it's a lothgate," said Harthor, "and presuming it leads back to Holc and not somewhere else. How do we activate it?"

"I have the means for that," said Goff, and I knew, by the fact he didn't elaborate, it would not be the same means by which we got here. I ran my eyes over his body, looking for magic, but though he gave off an aura, it was generalized. We wouldn't know what key he had till he was ready to use it.

"What do you mean, somewhere else?" asked Olenbry. "Are you saying these gates can lead anywhere?"

"To any other gate," corrected Harthor. "Of which there were many thousand at the height of the Empire, all the way from here to Ulaonnor Mor."

I shivered. The fabled capital of the Empire had been on the other side of the world. I had travelled the height and breadth of the Ilmar, and that was large enough. The Endlands were said to be a year's travel through desert, mountains, and oceans away from us.

"But," Harthor was saying, "when the Cataclysm occurred, the gates became fixed on their last destination. In theory." He looked at us all, ending with Goff. "Though no one has been able to generate enough arcana to make them work. Or so we thought."

Harthor had studied this with more than passing interest, it seemed.

"But are we still not sure," Rennielle asked, "whether the one at this place leads to Holc?"

Goff looked up at her and gave the old heart-melting smile I remembered from so many years ago.

"That's what we're here to find out."

"So," I summarized, "it takes us back to Holc. And I presume we have transport arranged from there. What if it takes us elsewhere? Or we can't activate it?"

He shrugged. "We walk."

I looked at the scale of the map. We were at least 150 leagues from the mountains that separated Oburakor from the Ilmar. It would be a very long walk into high mountain passes. Fortified ones at that.

It was a good day's march — about five leagues — from here to the temple marked on the map.

"In that case," I said, as a vestigial dust devil danced past us, scattering sand across the map, "we'd better get walking."

The march was long and tiring. We started out with small conversations, and I shifted amongst the file, learning more about my companions in snippets. But by midday the parched aspect of the land had worked its way into our mouths and throats, and talk had dried up like the water. It left me nothing to do but think: about Goff, and my grandfather, and the relationship between us all. Something about Goff's story didn't hold up.

We were such a strange crew to have assembled, with me added at the last hour. A task of such importance would be best planned for months, with a highly trained and well-informed body of operatives. 'Handpicked' in this instance seemed to mean no more than drawn like a fistful of multicoloured sweets from the apothecary's jar. We were all competent, trained with weapons, with varying degrees of military experience and a wide range of skills. Goff and Rennielle had a pre-existing relationship—and an antagonistic one at that—but Goff seemed to know the others by no more than name and reputation. And he seemed to know unreassuringly little about our mission.

I found myself questioning even more the wisdom of my grandfather in sending us on this strange quest, and Goff's wisdom for leading it. By the day's end, I'd decided to no longer leave my fate in the hands of men of dubitable ethics and mental capacity. Taking charge of the expedition would not be so hard. Safeguarding the fate of the Ilmar might be more difficult.

The temple came into view as a silhouette against a red and baleful couching sun.

"Is that it?" I asked Goff.

"Presumably so." He pulled out his map, fumbling with it.

I took one side and held it open for him, committing to memory all the details I could.

Judging by the map, a village once existed here but was now abandoned. Old wooden water flumes, like broken-backed dragons, snaked the desert we'd been marching, so once, it seemed, this dry soil had been farmed.

"With luck, there will be houses still standing or at least walls we can shelter in tonight," he pronounced.

I didn't think so. "Rennielle," I asked the Ilvani woman, "do you see any movement?"

Ilvani eyes are reputed to be sharper than ours, and my own father's blood made mine better than most as well. But I did not want to share that ... or the fact that along with movement, I could see an aura, even at this distance, of magic.

"Harthor," I continued, "what about magic?"

"Both," said Harthor, and Rennielle just nodded. "Unless we're certain of a friendly welcome, I doubt we'll be camping there tonight."

Goff shrugged. "A few Essaruk at most, according to our sources."

We all stared at him.

"We are not just a scouting party." He frowned. "We're a strike force too. Our job is to open that gate. Between us, we have the strength to overpower the small contingent there."

"Just go in and take the village by force?" asked Imerian. "Neither wise nor politic, I'd say."

"This is what you signed on to do," snapped Goff. I could see the unease beneath his scorn.

"I didn't sign anything," I pointed out. My voice was quiet but tinged with the authority I'd learned when working a crowded bar as a singer.

Goff rounded on me. "You came to the meeting. That is your mark."

I raised an eyebrow. "There are lawyers back in Rheran who would argue that, I'm sure. But first," I added, forestalling more argument, "we need to get there. I don't fancy taking an Essaruk village, or encampment, or group of religious fanatics, by force, sight unseen. I suggest we scout first."

Not a handful of Essaruk, not even a village's worth, but at least two hundred were encamped around the temple on the hill. Of those, at least 150 seemed to be soldiers or warriors of one sort, and there were a dozen or so priests, like the one we'd seen die in the keep, moving in and out of the temple itself. The rest were the usual mix of support and hangers-on an army needs and attracts. An army.

There seemed hardly any sentries, which made our job of watching from beside an old windmill easy. From our perch on the hill, we could see the movement in and out of the temple, and the pulse of arcane energy that thrummed and faded at intervals. I let Harthor describe it to us.

"It builds then fades," he said. "Almost as if they are attempting a magic they are not quite strong enough to hold on to."

"Is it the gate, do you think?" I ask.

"The type of aura definitely seems to signify a sort of translocation energy. But there is something more—transmutation, perhaps."

I wished I'd studied Carollus's dry books on arcana more thoroughly.

Harthor continued. "I could cast a spell to analyze it, but that would undoubtedly cause a ripple in its field, alerting the practitioners."

I shook my head. Discretion seemed more valuable than analysis at this point.

There was a larger movement. A squad of soldiers, around a dozen, surged forward and up the steps to the temple.

They entered in double file; the arcane glow blossomed and then faded.

Another dozen stepped forward: another burst of energy. And then another and another. That temple was not large enough to hold four score soldiers, and we all realized it. I looked at Harthor, about to comment, when a surge of arcana lit the night sky like fireworks, and a wind slammed into us with hurricane force. All went black for an instant, accompanied by the sensation of falling.

Darkness was the first thing I noticed, and then the cold. The next was the wind blowing the odour of burned hair, leather, and the smell my brain refused to identify as roast meat. I rolled over and felt rocky ground beneath me that tipped away like the deck of a ship at sea. It took a moment or two, holding onto the ground with my fingers and boot tips, to realize the ground did actually slope away, and its cant was not the product of dizziness. Of course. We had been on a hill. Was this still the same one? Or had another blast of arcana ripped us out of our place yet again?

I blinked, creating coloured spots before my eyes but nothing else. I heard movement to my left and reached out with one arm, unwilling still to sit up on what seemed an unstable incline. My hand encountered a boiled-leather pauldron that moved with the shoulder under it.

"Goffree." I coughed more than spoke the word.

"Are we still in Oburakor?" Olenbry's voice came from downslope.

"Damned if I know," said Harthor's.

"Imerian?" asked Goff, his voice even worse than mine.

"We are," confirmed the tree-priest, speaking as one who could no doubt taste it in the air or dirt or some such. The only one of our party who hadn't yet spoken was …

"Rennielle?" called Goff, and then louder. "Rennielle!"

I pushed myself to my knees, still searching the darkness. "Can anyone see anything?" I asked.

"As much as can be expected on a moonless night," replied Olenbry.

I heard Goff scramble to his feet beside me. "Where is that damned woman? Rennielle!" he called yet again.

"Hsst!" said Harthor. "Do you want to call the Essaruk down on us?"

Goff's feet sent pebbles fumbling downhill beside me as his voice retreated upslope. "It's black as Caradar's heart out here, but there's no sign of movement. Or the temple."

"Watch how you speak of the dead, lest you join them." Rennielle's icy voice emerged from the far left of us.

"Fingal's balls, woman. Where the hell have you been?"

"Looking," she said. "Which is what I'd encourage you to do if your Ilmarin eyes weren't so pathetic."

"My Ilvanin eyes can see nothing at all," grumbled Harthor. "Stop speaking in damned riddles. Why am I blind and you're not?"

I could envision her indifferent shrug though I couldn't see it. "Perhaps because I wasn't looking at the gate when it exploded."

"But I was," said Goff, "and I can see … as much as expected, at least, in this cursed dim starlight."

"Our eyes are less sensitive, thus less easily affected," said Imerian.

"Never mind why," I said. I had my own theory: that both Harthor and I had been using arcane sight when the explosion happened. "What happened? That felt like the same kind of … effect" —I chose my words carefully— "that landed us in Oburakor in the first place."

"The same but opposite," said Harthor. "I can't be sure, but I believe … that something caused the gate to malfunction. That the last thing through the gate was converted into pure arcana. And blown back this way."

"All those troops?" I asked.

"I doubt it. When a living being is converted into arcana, the energy is thousandfold. A beetle would be enough to cause a bonfire. Unless the destruction on the other side of the gate is far greater than here, I believe that was the result of a single Essaruk losing their life in transit. Had it been all the soldiers, it would have been a cataclysm the size of—"

"Ulaonnor Mor," I interrupted.

"Could that be the case on the other side of this gate?" asked Goff. "Wherever that is?"

We were all silent for half a dozen heartbeats.

"The glow leftover from Ulaonnor Mor," I said at last, "could be seen in the sky three hundred leagues away for years afterward." I didn't yet want to reveal my own blindness, so I waited. I heard Goff turn on the spot from atop the hill.

"If there were such a thing within three hundred leagues, it wouldn't be so blasted dark out here."

"Let's hope, then," said Imerian, "that no such thing has happened. If it had, we would pray for the souls of the departed. But if it didn't, there is a small army of Essaruk somewhere it wasn't earlier this evening. And perhaps we should find out where."

After a cold night in the blasted remains of the temple, we used the first grey light of morning to spread Goff's map out and study it—a frustrating exercise with a document so miserly in detail. My vision had returned, but with lingering spots of light and a headache worse than any I'd had in years.

The map bothered me. I acknowledged our mission was to fill in these details, but a sheaf of blank pages would have been nearly as useful and far less cumbersome than this large roll of aged vellum in its heavy tube. Why send a nearly useless but easily damaged antique into the wilds of Oburakor?

I hummed under my breath—something I did almost constantly when I might have to use my magic at a moment's notice but didn't want a sudden burst of song to be noticeable. I changed my cadence and shifted key, altering my own perception. And sure enough, faint tracings of pearlescent light began to show on the mostly blank parchment.

I stopped my song. The others needed to see this. "Harthor," I said, "Are there any arcane marks beyond what we can see now?"

He shook his head. "There is magic imbued in the vellum, that much I can tell, but it is a protective charm, not a translative one. I haven't been able to make the map reveal any further secrets."

Imerian nodded thoughtfully. "There are things human eyes can't parse. Markings on flowers, for instance, that only bees can see."

"How do you know that?" I asked.

"I can give myself the senses of other creatures—" He broke off at the meaningful tilt of my head and intoned a charm, or prayer perhaps. From his pack he retrieved a tiny vial of oil and touched a drop to the corner of each eye. When he opened them, he simply said "Oh."

"Oh what?" said Olenbry.

"It's covered in marks. But they make no sense. Here." He repeated his chant and touched each one of us with the oil.

The markings were indeed there—far stronger tracings than those I had seen on my own—but chaotic. They looked more like scribbles.

"Your ring," Harthor said to Goff.

Unusually compliant, Goff handed the ring to Harthor, who placed it in the centre of the map.

The arcane lines moved in a sickening motion, like a nest of vipers, resolving into something looking remarkably like a map. Only the words now were unreadable.

"It's ancient arcane script," breathed Harthor, "and these" —he pointed to symbols scattered around the map, "are lothgates. This, where we are," he said, moving the ring to another spot, which suddenly glowed green, "is an active loth-gate. I believe this map can show us which gates work and which are inactive."

He moved the ring around the map, and a pattern became clear. There were active gates dotted around Oburakor and dormant ones west of the mountains in the Ilmar.

"Well, that's a relief, then," said Olenbry. "Essaruk are moving around their own country at will but cannot come into the Ilmar, it seems."

"Except," said Goff, "that our leaders want to open the gates."

"But if a gate is open in the Ilmar, would that not allow Essa-ruk into your lands?" said Rennielle. Not 'our lands', I noticed, as I saw that no gate existed in the Valnirata.

"And us into theirs," said Goff. "The gates are a commercial and tactical advantage, and a risk at the same time."

"I assume there are safeguards," said Imerian.

"There's not a lock in the world that can't be picked, a key that can't be stolen," murmured Olenbry.

"Or a spell that can't be broken," finished Harthor. "Look at us," he said. "We are a handpicked team of specialists, skilled in both sorts of arcana needed to read this map, in espionage" —here he looked at Olenbry, who averted her eyes modestly— "tactics" —he addressed to Goff— "and … ?" He looked at me curiously.

"Lore," I said. "And pathfinding."

He nodded. "The only one who doesn't seem to have a purpose in this is you," he said, turning to Rennielle. "Are you just a hired weapon?"

She stood, and twitched her mouth into a thin smile. "I am here to make sure you fail."

§

Read the conclusion to Allaigna's Song: Oburakor *in* Pulp Literature *Issue 31, Summer 2021.*

THE ARTISTS

Kris Sayer
Cover artist, A Foundation of Lies

Kris Sayer has swum with dolphins, dived with sharks, hiked round 'Mount Doom', fixed a flat in the outback, eaten a ridiculous number of dumplings, and sketched more swords than you can shake an eleventh-century-blade-with-questionable-origins at. In between all those things, she's still made comics. *A Foundation of Lies* was originally the cover for her graphic novel *Sidequests*, and it features Tatterhood's goat Bokki, who first appeared in *Pulp Literature* (Issue 2, Spring 2014) in the story 'Unwanted Visitors'. You can find all of her illustrated tales at wealdcomics.com and pick up her comics and illustrations in *Pulp Literature* issues 1, 2, 5, 6, 10, 11, 15, 21, and 27.

Hugh Henderson
Artist, Blue Skies Over Nine Isles

Hugh Henderson is an artist and scholar based out of Vancouver, BC. He trains with both swords and pencils to master his arts, but still finds time to hang out with friends and prove to all that he is a massive nerd. He is inspired by the wide offerings of internet webcomics and paperbound graphic novels as well as cartoons and anime, and he hopes to inspire others with his work the same way. *Blue Skies Over Nine Isles* is an adventure on a new frontier featuring sinister robots and stylish heroes. Follow along at blueskiescomic.com.

MEL ANASTASIOU

In-house illustrator

Mel Anastasiou loves drawing for *Pulp Literature* because she loves the stories she illustrates. She draws in black and white, working from imagination and inspired by details from Renaissance compositions. You can find illustrations, writing tips, and news about her books and novellas at melanastasiou.wordpress.com, and see her artwork on Facebook at Bird and Branch Artwork.

Are you our next
writer-in-residence?

Applications now open
for 2022-23

Apply by Jan. 15, 2021

ucalgary.ca/cdwp

UNIVERSITY OF CALGARY
FACULTY OF ARTS
Calgary Distinguished Writers Program

MARKETPLACE

Books

Advent *by Michael Kamakana* • We thought we knew what the aliens wanted. Think again. • pulpliterature.com/advent

Allaigna's Song: Aria *by JM Landels* • The long-awaited sequel to the bestselling *Allaigna's Song: Overture.* •pulpliterature.com/allaignas-song

The Extra: A Monument Studios Mystery *by Mel Anastasiou* • Extra Frankie Ray gets her big break on the Silver Screen, until Murder steals the scene. pulpliterature.com/the-extra

The Labours of Mrs Stella Ryman: Further Fairmount Mysteries *by Mel Anastasiou* • Trapped in a down-at-the-heels care home. You'd be cranky too. • pulpliterature.com/stella-ryman-and-the-fairmount-manor-mysteries

What the Wind Brings *by Matthew Hughes* • Epic slipstream historical fiction • pulpliterature.com/product-category/novels/matthew-hughes

The Writer's Boon Companion *by Mel Anastasiou* • Thirty Days Towards an Extraordinary Volume • pulpliterature.com/subscribe/the-bookstore

Bookstores

Book Warehouse • 632 Broadway W, Vancouver, BC V5Z 1G1 • 604-872-5711 bookwarehouse.ca

Myth Hawker Travelling Bookstore • Canadian authors • Canadian content • small and independent press • mythhawker.ca

Phoenix On Bowen • 992 Dorman Rd, Bowen Island, BC V0N 1G0 • 604-947-2793

Village Books & Coffee House • 130-12031 First Ave, Richmond, BC V7E 3M1 • 604-272-6601 • villagebooks@shaw.ca

Western Sky Books • 2132-2850 Shaughnessy St, Port Coquitlam, BC V3C 6K5 • 604-461-5602 • store.westernskybooks.com

White Dwarf / Dead Write Books • 3715 10th Ave W, Vancouver, BC V6R 2G5 • 604-228-8223 • whitedwarf@deadwrite.com

Conferences and Events

Word on the Lake • May 2021 • Salmon Arm, BC • wordonthelakewritersfestival.com

Creative Ink Festival • May 2021 Burnaby, BC • creativeinkfestival.com

When Words Collide • August 2021 Calgary, AB • whenwordscollide.org

Wine Country Writers' Festival 24–25 September 2021 • Penticton, BC winecountrywritersfestival.ca

Surrey International Writers' Conference 22–24 October 2021 • Virtual Event • siwc.ca

Do you have a **story to tell?**
We can help!

Dreamers is dedicated to heartfelt writing. Visit our site for:

- Therapeutic Writing
- Poems & Stories
- Content Marketing
- Creative Nonfiction
- Writing Workshops
- Contests & Anthologies
- Residencies & Retreats
- ...and so much more!

www.DreamersWriting.com

DREAMERS
CREATIVE WRITING

GEIST
go to geist.com/subscribe
or call 1-888-GEIST-EH
Keep it weird.
Subscribe today!
GEIST
LOST CITY
FACT + FICTION • NORTH of AMERICA

on spec
the canadian magazine of the fantastic
Expect the unexpected.
www.onspec.ca

NEO-OPSIS
Science Fiction Magazine
www.neo-opsis.ca

PULP
Literature
Become a member!
Join the Pulp Literati today
pulpliterature.com/join-pulp-literati

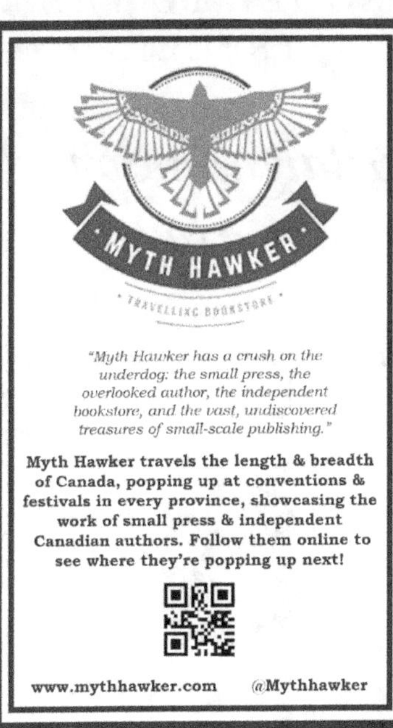

"Myth Hawker has a crush on the underdog: the small press, the overlooked author, the independent bookstore, and the vast, undiscovered treasures of small-scale publishing."

Myth Hawker travels the length & breadth of Canada, popping up at conventions & festivals in every province, showcasing the work of small press & independent Canadian authors. Follow them online to see where they're popping up next!

www.mythhawker.com   @Mythhawker

Allaigna's Song
Aria
JM Landels

Allaigna's Song
Overture
AMAZON #1 BESTSELLER
JM Landels

CONTESTS

Pulp Literature runs four annual contests for poetry, flash fiction, and short stories. For contest guidelines, prizes, and entry fees, see pulpliterature.com/contests.

The Bumblebee Flash Fiction Contest
Contest opens: 1 January 2021
Deadline: 15 February 2021
Winner notified: 15 March 2021
Winner published: Issue 31, Summer 2021
Prize: $300

The Magpie Award for Poetry
Contest opens: 1 March 2021
Deadline: 15 April 2021
Winner notified: 15 May 2021
Winner published: Issue 32, Autumn 2021
Prize: $500

The Hummingbird Flash Fiction Prize
Contest opens: 1 May 2021
Deadline: 15 June 2021
Winner notified: 15 July 2021
Winner published: Issue 33, Winter 2022
Prize: $300

The Raven Short Story Contest
Contest opens: 1 September 2021
Deadline: 15 October 2021
Winner notified: 15 November 2021
Winner published: Issue 34, Spring 2022
Prize: $300

$\mathcal{B}$ECOME A PATRON OF PULP LITERATURE

By supporting *Pulp Literature* on Patreon with \$2 or more per month, you will be laying the foundation for a secure future for the magazine, as well as ensuring that you never miss an issue! Your subscription includes four big issues of short stories, novellas, poetry, comics, and novel excerpts, delivered to your door or electronic mailbox each year. **Find us at patreon.com/pulplit**

If you prefer to subscribe through our website, go to pulpliterature. com/subscribe.

Or you can send a cheque with the form below to
Subscriptions, Pulp Literature Press, 21955 16 Ave, Langley BC, V2Z 1K5, Canada

- -

Don't miss an issue!

- ❑ **Send me 2 years (8 issues) at the special rate of \$90** (save \$30)*
- ❑ **Send me 1 year (4 issues) for \$50** (save \$10)*
- ❑ **Send me 2 years of digital issues for \$30** (save \$9.92)
- ❑ **Send me 1 year of digital issues for \$17.50** (save \$2.47)

Name: ____

Address: ____

City: _________________________________ Prov. / State: __________

Postal code: ______________ Country:_____________________

Email: ____

- ❑ Payment enclosed
- ❑ Bill me
- ❑ New
- ❑ Renewal

Make cheques payable in Canadian funds to J. Landels. Include email address for digital editions and Paypal billing, or subscribe at www.pulpliterature.com.

*for postage outside Canada add \$20 per year in North America or \$36 per year overseas.